THE WISHBOURNE CANDLES

THE WISHBOURNE CANDLES

When Carey Constable discovers that her beloved mother is not related to her at all, she is so shocked she takes the first job the agency offers without questioning why something so well-paid hasn't been snapped up long ago. When she arrives at the ancient mansion of Wishbourne Towers she senses evil in the atmosphere. She learns about the glowing apparition of a candelabra with seven lit candles – the ghost which is said to appear before disaster is visited on the Holford family – and feels the terrible force of love for Simon Holford, sometimes so tender and devoted, sometimes a man to fear.

The Wishbourne Candles

by

Delia Foster

Dales Large Print Books
Long Preston, North Yorkshire,
BD23 4ND, England.

British Library Cataloguing in Publication Data.

Foster, Delia
  The Wishbourne candles.

  A catalogue record of this book is
  available from the British Library.

  ISBN   978-1-84262-837-9 pbk

First published in Great Britain 1972 by
Robert Hale & Company

Copyright © Delia Foster 1972

Cover illustration © Stephen Carroll by arrangement with
Arcangel Images

The moral right of the author has been asserted

Published in Large Print 2011 by arrangement with
The Executor of Delia Foster, care of S. Walker Literary Agency

Dales Large Print is an imprint of Library Magna Books Ltd.

Printed and bound in Great Britain by
T.J. (International) Ltd., Cornwall, PL28 8RW

Chapter One

The rain slashed against the windows of the compartment as my train streaked through wild Devon country towards the coast, and although it was late Spring, it might have been a November day, it was so dark and menacing. I was about as depressed as could be. The weather couldn't do much for me, nor the stark landscape. Nothing of it made sense. I had agreed to come on this journey without thinking much about it because I had still been so stunned by what had happened at home. I don't think I really began to come out of that frozen shell until the only other person in the compartment alighted at the junction, and I was left alone. And then I asked myself, what was I doing, coming down to this little-known spot, without having stopped to think why a resident job like this should still be open, when it had been so well-paid.

The agency had offered it to me rather tentatively, I remembered. I could see the face of that person who offered the job to me;

a typical business-woman's face. Shrewd, keen to assess the other person, knowledge-able as to how far she could go. In no time at all, she had out of me the reason for my wanting a resident job at all.

'So,' she said, 'I am to understand that your mother is intending to marry again, and go abroad with her new husband, sell-ing up your home.'

'You sound as if you approve of that!' I couldn't help saying rather sharply, for she was smiling in a satisfied way.

'Let's say, my dear,' she said, with a wry smile, 'that no resident job is perfect, but the applicant more likely to try to make a "go" of it, is the one who hasn't a cosy home background beckoning. Too many girls get homesick and throw up a resident job that might, with a bit of patience, have turned out quite well.'

That was only too true, I reflected, and as she pulled a form towards her and began to fill it in with my details, I wondered what she would have said if she could have known what had happened at home to make me decide to go as far away as possible from that quiet town up north, and all my friends – people who had known me since, when? Not since my birth, I reflected unhappily, but certainly from my babyhood.

I heard myself giving details to that elegant person with the superb self-confidence, behind the agency desk. 'Carey Constable, aged twenty-two, unmarried,' and as I watched her write it down, I thought of the boy-friends I had had, and wondered what any of them would have said if they had known what I had just recently discovered.

A description had to go on this form. 'Grey eyes,' she murmured, with a swift glance. 'Brown hair. Did you bring a recent photograph with you? Ah, yes,' and she took it from me and with a quick appraising glance, compared it with my face, and no doubt decided that that short brown crop with the thick fringe, and the pale almost unmade up face wasn't going to disturb the household I was about to go into, nor to wreck the hopes of its women folk where their men were concerned. Clean and neat and rather utilitarian was my appearance. I had never been able to get madly interested in good grooming, being the outdoor type. 'Height five feet four, slender build. What do you weigh?' and when I told her, she entered that, with a frown, no doubt thinking I was under-weight and wouldn't last the course on health grounds.

Then she briefed me. 'This job is on the

coast,' she began, carefully choosing her words. 'Not an attractive part of the coast, I am afraid, but then you're going to work there, not to take a long holiday,' and she smiled to sweeten the words. 'It's a very big old house, but several members of the family need the services of a secretary, so you'll be kept pretty busy. The trouble is, they all work very odd hours, and most girls nowadays like regular hours and regular times off. If you aren't likely to make a fuss on that point, you may find just what you're looking for, because it's not badly paid,' and she promptly took my breath away with the salary offered.

But I didn't query it. I just sat there thinking about my mother when she had told me she was marrying again, and so the moment went by when I should have asked, why all that much money for just a resident typist?

I thought of my mother, much the same height and colouring as myself, the outdoor type, too. We had been so close. We went for long walks together, and when she had learned to drive, I had, too, and we amicably shared the small second-hand car. We liked dogs and exercised and groomed them and in holiday times we had 'obliged' neighbours and friends by taking in their animals while they were away. How could two people look reasonably alike (as to height and colouring that is) and share the same tastes and the same depth of affection, and yet be miles and miles apart?

I didn't remember Horace Constable. He was the man my mother referred to as 'your father'. 'Your father would have liked to see you now,' or 'Your father always wanted you and me to be close friends,' and then from the wide circle of our friends, Tom Brewster had emerged, and had edged his way into our lives. One thing I didn't share with my mother and that was her love of whist, so it seemed natural that Tom should play cards with her while I exercised the dogs in the evening, or while I went to the club to be with young people of my own age. I should have seen what was coming. She was young enough to want to re-marry.

It was a blow, but I didn't mind it all that much, not even when she admitted that he wanted to go back to Canada and take her with him. I think if it could have stayed as she had wanted it to be, I would have been happy enough to accept the new order of things. I wouldn't have been possessive about her. But her new husband-to-be wasn't likely to know that, I suppose. That last day I was at home, he had been to tea and said, 'Did you tell her, Phyllis?'

My mother had looked so distressed, I wondered what on earth had been going on. 'Tell me what?' I demanded.

'No, Tom, tonight, I thought,' my mother had pleaded.

He had got up with impatience, and a little anger, too. 'No, you won't. You'll put it off again. And I know what it'll be! We'll go to Canada and she'll be resentful of me taking you off, or else she'll be always wanting to come out and visit us.'

'Tom!' My mother had pleaded, but he wouldn't listen.

'I'm a plain man,' he had said to me. 'I like to think I can call a spade a spade. If you'd been her own daughter I could have understood it, but you're not. You're no relation at all. Adopted, that's all. There, now you've had it straight, and you'll not feel so bad about her going off and leaving you, will you?'

I didn't even look at him. I just looked at Phyllis Constable, who for all of my life had been not only my mother but my closest confidante and friend, and I couldn't believe it. If only she had told me herself, not left this stranger to do it! Or better still, why couldn't she have married him and gone away, leaving me to always think I was hers? It wouldn't have mattered to him surely!

The voice of the woman at the agency cut across my thoughts. 'Now before you sign this form, just have another think. Are you sure you want to go to Wishbourne Towers?'

'Quite sure,' I said, with tight lips. I had walked out of the place that had been my home without another word. I hadn't taken anything, not a thing; just my coat on the way through the hall. There was very little that had once belonged to me, that I could feel was mine; that I could feel that man my mother was marrying wouldn't comment on. I wanted nothing from either of them, and this, a job offered to me almost at once, was manna from heaven! 'Quite sure,' I said again, and I almost missed the flicker of relief over her face.

Well, if the surrounding countryside was anything to go by, then I wasn't surprised that no-one wanted to stay. It was growing dark now, and a cold little wind licked at me as I got off the train at a place called Happington. I looked at my watch to check the time, and saw only a white place on the brown of my wrist, where my watch had been. Gold, on a nice expanding bracelet, it had been a birthday gift, and I had had to sell it to scrape together the barest necessities to constitute 'luggage'. I walked till I found the station clock. The train had arrived late. On a wet night at the back of beyond, I don't really think I had expected anything else. I went outside to find a bus of sorts, and saw instead an ancient Rolls, driven by a lean elderly man.

Never has a vehicle looked so inviting. The rain dripped down my neck and from the brim of my hat. My feet felt damp already. I stood staring wistfully at the driver, who stared steadily back, and when I had plucked up courage to ask if I could beg a lift up front, a man shot out of the station, and wrenched open the back door of the Rolls.

In the light of the one lamp in the station yard, I saw a young man, tall, well-made, improbably handsome. His crisp waving hair glistened with the rain, but he had a good new raincoat, whose stand-up collar had a no-nonsense look about it. Briefly I envied him that good new raincoat.

He saw me and hesitated. Then his whole face lit in a good-natured smile, and he called, 'Want a lift?'

I squelched over to the car. 'Oh, I'd love

14

one, but I'm going to Wishbourne Towers. Is that on your way?'

The driver muttered over his shoulder, but the young man ignored him. 'I'm going there, too,' he said, and stood back for me to get in, but the old man in front said something and pointedly opened his door, so I took the hint and got in beside the driver. After all, I was only staff, wasn't I? The young man grinned and closed his door, and we drove out of the yard, sedately, the driver bristling with anger and disapproval.

The young man leaned back. I could see his amused grin in the mirror. 'You appear to be rather damp,' he remarked. 'What are *you* going to Wishbourne for? Not a guest?' he frowned. 'I thought it was to be a so called quiet week-end.'

'So 'tis,' the driver put in, in a surly tone. 'This here will be the young woman from the typing agency. Was expected.'

I endorsed that, with dignity. I had, after all, only begged a lift. There was no need for the driver to be so up-stage about it.

'At least, Logsden,' the young man said irritably. 'It's the least we could do to give the lady a lift on a night like this. May I introduce myself,' he said pleasantly, to me. 'I am Holford of Wishbourne.'

I saw the driver glance up sharply to the mirror where no doubt he could see the man in the back seat, but he said nothing. I, however, cursed my bad luck. This must be my new boss, and very grand he made himself sound, too, and here I was, like a wet hound, looking at my very worst, and starting my new career with begging a lift!

I stammered, 'Oh, I didn't know. I'm sorry. I'm Carey Constable. I wouldn't have – well, there isn't a bus.'

'Think nothing of it! And don't start out by apologizing. That will get you nowhere at Wishbourne, will it, Logsden?' and he laughed.

Logsden muttered, 'You didn't ought to have, Master Simon – you know her ladyship doesn't hold with–' but the young man cut him off pretty sharply.

'Leave me to tackle Lady Isadora,' he said curtly. To me, he added, 'No doubt you haven't met my aunt but don't listen to Logsden. She's a charming person. But there, he paints everyone in my family as an ogre. You just form your own opinion, Miss Carey Constable – as I've no doubt you will, if that determined little chin is anything to go by!'

'Master Simon, you didn't ought–' the driver insisted.

16

'Good heavens, man, what do you expect me to do? Throw her out into the road in this downpour, to walk on foot to the Towers? To blazes with the legend, let's be human for heaven's sake!'

'Legend?' I asked sharply. 'May I ask what you mean?'

'Oh, there I go! Letting it out to another stranger! Well, you'll hear it soon enough, I suppose, but I suspect it was created by someone in the family who didn't approve of the current fashion of hitch-hiking. The saying goes that if one of us gives a lift to a stranger, the candles are seen. It's much the same as the legend among sailors, that if a ship picks up someone out of the sea, one of the crew dies.'

'Candles?' I fastened on the one word, and looked round at him. The driver made noises of disapproval, but the young man lounging easily in the back seat wasn't to be put off. Looking at him I couldn't believe that he'd be afraid of anything, least of all a legend.

'The candles,' he repeated gravely. 'The Wishbourne Candles. You might say it's our ghost, our bit of haunting. A seven-branched candelabra appears, with every candle lit, and there's supposed to be a death or disaster in the family soon after. Personally I've never seen it–'

'Master Simon!' Logsden moaned from the front seat.

The young man laughed softly. 'There's one who won't sleep tonight for sheer terror,' he told me. And to Logsden, he said briskly, 'Don't be so lily-livered, man! It won't happen to you! It only happens to a Holford, and if I'm not afraid, why should you be?'

'You're not afraid of nothing, Master Simon! That's half your trouble! And what her ladyship will say, I don't know!' He leaned out of his window, turned slickly considering the length of the car, and we were going uphill, and in the light of the headlamps I got my first glimpse of Wishbourne. A knobbly outer wall, and rising above it, old stone walls, deep-set shadowed windows like the sockets of eyes, a muddle of small steep roofs, very tall twisty chimneys, towers, bays and buttresses, and then the whole structure vanished into the darkness as the car reached level ground and the headlamps were dipped.

'Wishbourne Towers,' the young man in the back said, quietly, and there was pride and quiet pleasure in his tones, and some-

18

thing else that I couldn't quite understand. A warning? No, not quite that, but something else apart from the more pleasant things he might be feeling about his home. My practical mind thought he might perhaps be dwelling on the cost of its upkeep, the dreadful question of staff (of which I heard a lot at the agency!) and perhaps the situation of the house, because now the car had stopped, the shutting off of the engine and wind-screen wipers let in another sound: the hiss and thunder of the sea, somewhere surprisingly near, and down below. This, then, must be a dwelling on the cliffs, I thought, with a shudder, as a gust of rain swept across and drenched me as I got out of the car.

'Welcome to Wishbourne!' a mocking voice said at my elbow, as the young man from the back of the car stretched his long length and strode off through a tall gateway.

The driver said in a surly tone, 'Here's your case!' and almost threw it out at my feet, and prepared to drive off until I called out to him: 'Where shall I go?'

He said politely enough, 'In at that door,' and jerked an expressive thumb, and then he, too, drove the big car out of sight and I was left in semi-darkness, on cobbles in a courtyard that was almost medieval.

But in the house it was warm enough, bright enough, and a woman in a tweed skirt and wool twin set, who said she was the housekeeper, took me to a sort of utility room at the back, where I stripped off my wet outer things. 'Come and see her ladyship first,' the housekeeper said, 'then I'll show you your room. Is this all you brought? Ah, well, they don't stay. I suppose they warned you at the agency.'

For the first time I was thankful about that aspect. It saved me having to explain my limited wardrobe. I followed her out into the enormous flagged hall and down what seemed miles of corridor. I was suddenly tired. Tired and cold and hungry. Since my precipitate leaving of my home, I hadn't eaten much. I was suddenly conscious of a gnawing hunger, which, I supposed, was the prime cause of the feeling of apprehension which had clutched at me ever since I had entered the Rolls at Happington.

I don't know what I expected to find in 'her ladyship' after the driver's remarks and the first sight of this house, which was not my idea of a home at all. It smelt like an old church or an ancient museum. Is it the stonework that smells so oddly, suggesting great age and times long past? Or is it the woodwork? Perhaps I'm suggestive to such things, though I wouldn't have said so, but the fanciful notion took me, as I followed the very modern housekeeper through the corridors of Wishbourne that evening, that all the people who had ever lived under that roof were there, invisible, in the shadows, looking at me and wishing me anything but well. Perhaps it was the story of the candles.

I don't know. Whatever it was, I certainly didn't expect to find the sort of person who was waiting for me in a room that was not much different from the brisk and business-like office at the employment agency. Indeed, the Lady Isadora was very much like that well-groomed business woman who had persuaded me to take this job. Like her to the extent that she favoured a light tweedy sort of dress, plain and very well-cut, and a few pieces of good solid jewellery that really was gold, and really contained diamonds. Beyond that, her manner was arrogant with a thin layer of pleasantness, just right for the big boss handing out work and not expecting much service. She said, 'Oh, there you are! You'll be,' (and here she consulted a letter, presumably from the Agency), 'Carey Constable, yes? Well, Carey, let's hope you can type. The last one

21

couldn't. We call the girls by their Christian names – less trouble than memorizing surnames. They don't stay long. We've had three Margarets, four Anns, one Miranda, one Pearl, and a bristling elderly Harriet. Let's see what you can get done in a week before you bustle off,' and she turned her attention to a big filing tray.

'This stuff needs two carbons. My speeches for the next week. Hope you can read my writing. If you can't, have an inspired guess – it'll probably be better than the original effort. I go off a bit when I'm tired. Now this stuff,' and she turned to another tray, 'I can't tell you much about. It's my brother's work. Do you best with it. It's manuscript – needs one carbon – Sir Hilton was in the Navy and is writing his memoirs. Query anything you think is too outrageous or indiscreet, and when he emerges from the King's Room, grab him and make him answer all your questions.'

'Yes, ma'am,' I said rather faintly, for the desk was still piled with a mountain of papers.

'Those are bills. Leave 'em till we get some money in from somewhere,' she said carelessly. 'You won't have time to do anything with 'em, anyway, because my brother Rex will want to give you shorthand notes. He's an historian and does articles for the Sunday press so he'll rush you. I'd resist his pressure, if I were you, but give him to think he's your favourite boss, that's if you decide you can stay. But remember, my work comes first!'

She looked at me then, and appeared surprised by what she saw. So far I'd just been another pair of hands to work on a typewriter. 'Good heavens, not much of you! Have you been starving? Better clear off and find some food. There's always plenty, though I can't think how. And chase Kidby to give you a decent room.'

'Kidby?' I murmured.

'The housekeeper,' she said impatiently, and waved a hand of dismissal at me.

She had boomed in an elegant voice like a leading lady on a London stage and now it was quiet, deadly quiet but for the rustle of papers, as she searched for something. I went out, wondering what Sir Hilton and her brother Rex were like.

The great hall was deserted. Where would I find Miss Kidby, for heaven's sake? And then a man came out of a room on the right. I caught a glimpse of book-lined walls and a grand piano. Even at that distance there was no mistaking the young man who had insisted on giving me a lift in the Rolls. I went up to him, meaning to ask him my way about.

'I've just seen your Aunt Isadora,' I began, and then I noticed he had dark glasses on.

He stopped and stared down at me, then took them off. I hadn't made a mistake. It was the same handsome face, topped by the crisp waving fair hair, above the straight brown brows but the beautifully shaped mouth was now unsmiling, and there was a chilling hostility in those brown eyes, as he stared down at me and said, with every evidence of never having seen me before, 'Who the blazes are you?'

Chapter Two

I thought he meant that I shouldn't presume to be jolly with him, on the strength of a lift in the car. I said, 'I'm sorry, but you're the only one I know here. I only wanted to ask how I could find the housekeeper. Once I find her, I can manage.'

His cynical glance raked me from top to toe and he said, 'When and where am I supposed to have made your acquaintance?'

'Well perhaps you don't call offering me a lift making my acquaintance,' I snapped heatedly. I was quite sure now that, like the others before me, I wasn't going to like being here. 'I'm sorry I spoke to you, sir,' and with exaggerated accent on the last word I turned and decided to try every door until I found someone else I could ask. This was ridiculous!

'I have never offered a young woman a lift in my life,' he said coldly, 'and I'd be obliged if you don't repeat that story. Who are you, anyway?'

'The newest typist,' I said, equally coldly.

'I see,' he said, and with frigid politeness, he said, 'Then I will show you how to find the housekeeper,' and he went across to the far wall and tugged at a bell rope. I hadn't noticed it and I wouldn't have presumed to use it. It was an intimidating sort of bell-rope. But he tugged it with venom, and when the housekeeper came, he said, with biting pleasantness, 'Kidby, you are neglecting your duties. You have mislaid one of my aunt's lambs. Do something about it, will you?'

Miss Kidby clucked in annoyance and twittered with apology and took me by the arm and led the way to the back stairs where we effaced ourselves. My last view of the turncoat was standing in lone splendour in the middle of that vast hall, slowly and with dignity replacing his dark glasses.

'Who was that?' I demanded, preparing to kick myself if I had mistaken him for someone else, but no, I couldn't have done, for she said at once, 'That was Mr Simon, you know. Oh, her ladyship thinks the world of him!'

'I can't think why,' I said tartly. 'I was just wondering how I could find you, Miss Kidby, since her ladyship ordered me to. No-one helps anyone around here, do they?'

'It's because there have been so many typists,' she soothed. 'We were all very helpful with the first one or two, but they came and went so quickly, and I expect Mr Simon got rather bored with being helpful to strangers. Never mind, dear, I expect you and I will get on like a house afire. Now first of all, do remember to use the back stairs. Her ladyship is very special about only the family and their friends using the grand staircase. Then, don't use the bells, or Mr Rex will get in a state. And if Sir Hilton wants to tell you some long involved story, it's wiser to stand and listen. That's advice only – you aren't forced to take it.'

Still, it was advice I was glad to take. I could see that the moment I met Sir Hilton. A large man, bluff, florid, confident that anyone first seeing him would recognize the daring old sea dog and only too willing to tell improbable sea stories in which he had come out with full flying honours, he decided to pounce on me with glee and tell me he was sure that I wouldn't be like the others.

'What's your name, gal?' he demanded, and didn't wait to hear. 'Where do you come from, eh?' and when I began to tell him, he cut in with the remark that he couldn't stand

27

people from further north than Birmingham but that no doubt I had not been there very long and really hailed from the south. Having delivered himself of that, he started to tell me how he came to be writing his memoirs, but unfortunately Rex Holford came in.

'What the devil do you mean by interrupting me, sir, without so much as a by-your-leave?' Sir Hilton howled. 'Can't you see I'm working, heh?'

Mr Rex was a thin scholarly type, and tried looking at me without his glasses and then with them. 'Hah,' he pronounced, after some thought, 'this appears to be yet another young person from the secretarial agency. Let us this time have a rota so that one might partake of fair shares of her services, h'm?'

'Fair shares, yes,' Sir Hilton agreed. 'You hogged the last one to yourself, so this one's mine, and that's right!'

I ventured to say something. 'Lady Isadora has already given me a lot of work to be done for everyone,' I said, adding meaningly, 'accumulated work.' I played with the idea of telling them that she had said her work came first and then decided against it. 'I think I'd better get on with that, in alphabetical order,' I said at last, on inspiration.

Sir Hilton smiled brilliantly, but Mr Rex said glumly, 'But that puts me last!'

'But I'll stay up late doing yours, sir, to make up,' I pacified him, and for the moment all was well.

Miss Kidby rescued me in the long, long corridor from the King's Room, and took me to see the room that would be mine.

It was huge. I said, 'Couldn't I have a smaller room, one that's easier to keep warm?'

'They all sleep here, the typists,' she said earnestly. 'It's very good of Lady Isadora to let them have a big guest room like this. The only small ones are on the floor above, but I do agree they're easier to heat. Come and see,' and she took me to one reached by a spiral staircase at the end of the corridor, and which was reasonably out of reach of everyone.

'I could work here, couldn't I?' I said. 'It's only a portable typewriter. I noticed it. Then I wouldn't be interrupted. I often work at night, quite late.'

She looked at me with new interest.

She said slowly, 'Well, of course, if that's how you go on, then you won't find this job so hard as the others did. Let's see if we can make you nice and snug. It's a corner room, and you'll hear the wind a lot, but the walls are strong.'

'I know. I noticed they were of knobbly stone,' I agreed.

'But of course they keep the place very dry. I'll find you a bigger electric fire. Thank goodness the place has been freshly wired up. The last young woman complained that she had nowhere to keep her books and belongings, so I expect you'd like another bookcase.'

As she seemed so obliging, I thought I might as well take advantage of it while she was in the mood. I had nowhere else to go, so I was determined, in my heart, to stay here as long as I could. I made a little list, which impressed her. She was, I found, fanatically tidy. In no time at all, she had brought up to me a really big electric fire, an electric blanket for the small single bed, a bookcase and a cupboard, and a table with drawers that would serve to work at. She said she would find thicker curtains for the window the next day, when it was lighter to see to put them up. The room looked absolutely different and surprisingly snug.

'I expect you'd like your supper brought up here,' she said, 'but to be honest I don't think I'd get anyone to bring it all this way up. It's just as difficult to keep maids as it is secretaries.'

'Would you mind if I brought it up on a tray?' I asked her. 'Then if it's sandwiches, I can be going through the work I've been given while I'm eating.'

'My, you *are* a demon for work,' she observed, and suddenly she smiled, a really big warm smile that lit her face. 'So am I really.'

I can't imagine what the other secretaries had got up to, but my passion for work and keeping out of sight soon endeared me to the family.

Lady Isadora said, 'Good heavens, girl, all that work and not a mistake? What's the matter with you?' and when I looked surprised at that, she shrugged and said, 'Can't think why you didn't get snapped up in London, if you're all that good.'

It seemed an ungrateful way on her part of looking at it but I suppose it was mainly surprise, for the two uncles said much the same thing, in their different ways. Sir Hilton asked frankly, 'What's the catch, young woman? You're no more interested in my work than that doorknob is.'

'Then it isn't any use my saying I am, is

it?' I said reasonably. 'But I am interested in having a lot of work to do, being kept occupied all the time, and being able to work in my own little corner and being left alone.'

I smiled as I said it, to take away any sting the words might have been thought to have. He sat back in his chair, eased his portly frame into a comfortable position, and said, 'H'm. Suppose it means a man in it somewhere. Jilted, I shouldn't wonder.'

It struck me that it might be a good thing to let him think that. I didn't answer, but waited for his stream of work he had dictated the day before, for when I should have finished the other lot. Where the work was concerned, we got on well. The only thing I couldn't stand was having to waste time listening to his sea dog stories.

Not that Mr Rex was any easier to get on with. He was, if possible, even more suspicious when he found that I got everyone's work done on time.

'Suppose you won't be staying,' he said gloomily, and when I said I thought it highly likely that I would be, he positively beamed at me.

It was Mr Rex who told me about the Cave of Gold. I suppose he wanted to reward me in some way for getting all his back-log of work done. I can't believe it was for any malicious reason.

He told me it was at the northern end of our own beach. 'Seen the beach at all yet?' he barked.

I said I hadn't.

'What, been here almost a week and not seen the beach yet? This won't do, child! Exploiting you, that's what everyone is!' As if he wasn't doing his share of exploiting, I thought, with a smile.

I hadn't even been shown over the house yet, which I should have liked a lot more. But the front was denied to me, because of not being allowed on the Grand Staircase. The best I could do was to slip out of the back, between bouts of work, and walk all round, looking up at the great sinister pile and trying to imagine what lay behind those walls and the windows that looked like sightless eyes.

'You ought to get some fresh air,' Sir Hilton told me severely, lifting me shamelessly from Mr Rex by way of another pile of work. 'Don't listen to him if he's telling you about caves. Take my advice and walk inland. Very pretty walks inland.'

'I have been to the village and a mile or two beyond,' I told him but he pooh-poohed this. 'You should get up at five, child, and do a ten mile walk before breakfast.'

'I would like to, sir, but I don't know how to get out of the house at that hour.'

That made him laugh and he told me of a way. A small door out of the passage running behind the library. For some reason it was only bolted at the bottom at night and the bolt was well-oiled. All the other doors in the house were locked by the staff when they went to bed and the keys taken away. If the family were coming in late they could get in without waking the staff.

I went out next morning. The door opened into a small closed place with high walls; the one-time herb garden. Neglected now, it led into other enclosed gardens, the walls high and built of the knobbly local stone. I thought what a pity it was that nobody seemed to bother with them. They would have been excellent forcing places, sheltered as they were from the sea by the bulk of Wishbourne Towers itself and I had visions of strawberries, tomatoes, marrows... My mind ran on, and I pleasurably wandered through until I came out into a lane, narrow, stifling below high tangled hedges, and this went downwards, through a tangle of blackberries, to the beach.

It was a beautiful place, wild and lovely. The fine sand was strewn with great boulders smoothed by the tides, with little pools at their base. It was ridiculous, I know, but I took off my shoes and stockings and paddled happily. The air was cold but still, and the water curiously warm. Baby crabs vanished into the still wet sand and even the gulls weren't making a noise yet. The sun was creeping up over the rim of the horizon, bathing everything with an unearthly pinkish golden light, and even the gaunt, rugged cliffs took on sheer beauty at this deserted hour of the day.

I suppose if I had been using my eyes, I would have seen the hoofmarks in the sand, going back the way I had come, but I had eyes only for the sky and cliffs, so I wasn't prepared for the sudden tumult of horse and rider behind me. They came on me so suddenly, I couldn't think, even afterwards, where they had been. I skipped out of the way in time, to see Simon tear past, on a big black horse. Considering he had the whole of the beach, it seemed pointedly rude to come so close.

He had, of course, been wearing dark glasses, and I wondered then if the truth was that he couldn't see very well, but I decided that he would have to be blind indeed not to see one solitary person on the whole deserted beach.

He was waiting for me, where the caves started. I didn't see him at first. He was leaning against a rock, watching me with an amused expression, because I had found the caves. Cave after cave, not exactly pitting the cliff base, but hiding themselves in clefts and folds, so that they weren't immediately obvious to the naked eye. I was enchanted. Then I heard him laugh.

'What do you mean by almost riding me down?' I demanded. I was still smarting over that incident.

He didn't stop smiling exactly, but there was a change in his face, as if he were forming the correct reply to that. 'What am I supposed to have ridden you down on?' he asked.

'That big black horse. Surely you had enough room without wanting the bit I was walking on?'

'Oh, that,' he said. 'Sorry, m'dear, but that is a rogue animal who likes to go where he will. Were you hurt?'

'No. You can see I'm not,' I said, puzzled. He didn't seem to know much about it. Well, of course, if he were like me, he might have been in a day-dream, not expecting anyone to be there. But it was rather odd.

'Then why the fuss?' he said lazily.

'It scared me, that's all. How would you like to be walking on an apparently deserted beach and be frightened out of your life by a big black horse coming up behind you?'

He said he understood and apologized. 'Must have been miles away,' he said ruefully. 'Look, m'dear, don't mention it up at the house, eh? Don't say you saw me at all. You see, the thing is, they like me to be dead serious, and it gets rather boring. I'm a fun-loving lad at heart, so I get away when I can. But you know what they're like – questions, questions, all the time. Get me?'

That seemed the first reasonable explanation I'd had so far. 'Yes, I understand, sir,' I allowed, 'but there isn't any need to bite my head off when I speak to you, is there?'

'I don't know,' he grinned. 'If you come up to me and accuse me of giving lifts to young ladies, in the hearing of the uncles, or the aunt, what do you expect?'

I shrugged. That, of course, was true, except that I had thought nobody was about.

Almost at once, he said, 'Never mind your troubles, lass, want to see the caves? I suppose you've heard of the Cave of Gold, though why it's considered special I can't think. It has no gold that I ever discovered and heaven knows, I searched for it enough when I was a nipper. Here it is,' and he pointed to a rather deeper inlet.

I was so surprised at his change of mood, but I thought it wiser not to comment on it. One thing still bothered me, however. 'What have you done with your horse?'

'Don't worry, you won't have it come up behind you again,' he said. Which seemed to imply that he had both tethered it safely and that I was being rather inquisitive. I shrugged and let the point go, and I was glad, because he turned out to be the most entertaining companion.

He took me up the length of the cave. It was steep, narrow, rough going underfoot, but it widened out into a sort of chamber where there was a table and chair of sorts, and an oaken chest.

'We brought those here, years ago, to play with. What kids will do for fun,' he said, a trace of nostalgia in his voice.

'We?' I took him up.

He grinned at me and touched my chin with one finger. 'We – the person I played with in my wicked boyhood,' he teased, refusing to tell me just who. 'Did you never play on the beach when you were young?' he asked me, lazily sitting down on the chest and pointing to the chair.

The place smelt of stale seaweed, the sharp acrid smell of ozone, tarry rope, old rotten wood. It had an element of adventure and fun about it, as it must have had for two boys, long ago. I said, 'Yes, I did, but it wasn't a wild beautiful beach like this. It was a sort of bathing-hut and sandcastle beach, crowded.'

'Oh.' He pulled a face of disgust. 'Give me the empty places of this wonderful earth. I know another beach further up. Want to come one morning?'

With a wary eye on the time, I allowed that I would like to. 'How do we get there, and what would your family say if they found out?'

'They won't, of course,' he said, his smile fading, 'and I have a small craft, outboard motor. Could be fun, that's if you'd care for it.'

Reason warned me to refuse. He wasn't to be trusted. He blew hot and cold, even though he had given a good excuse for that. But I wanted to go with him. He had a radiance when he was smiling. An easy happy-go-lucky nature, and a magnetism about him that I couldn't resist.

'All right, I'd love to go, if you're sure it will be all right.'

'Now just what do you mean by "all right"?' he teased. 'Your personal safety, your moral safety, or a lack of faith in my ability to entertain you or cover up for you in the bosom of the family.'

'All, I should say,' I flashed, with hot cheeks.

He threw a friendly arm round me for an instant.

'You're a sport,' he said firmly. 'Look here, if I've snapped at you or done anything you didn't expect, I'm sorry. The staff complain of it so it isn't likely I'd leave you out, when I'm letting people feel the rough edge of my tongue. Forgive?'

Forgive! I'd have forgiven him anything when he was in that mood.

'Why is this called the Cave of Gold?' I asked him as we came out into the sunshine. The sun was almost completely up now, and there was a sharp little wind brisking up. White horses were on the sea, which was now running in, and he said, 'Not smugglers or pirates or wreckers, be assured of that. Just a legend that one of my family hid his gold there when the throne changed hands.

People did in those days, I'm told. Plenty of us have searched for it since, but I expect someone else got there before us.'

'What an odd place to hide anything. Obvious, I would have thought,' I said crossly.

'No,' he said slowly. 'They do say, in the village, that one cave had a sort of natural closing to it at high tide. A kind of rocking stone. I suppose if that were so, the family could have devised some way of making it work if the officials came searching. I don't know.' And then he lost interest in it.

'I ought to get back,' I said, looking at my watch.

As I stepped out of the cave on to the beach, I thought I heard, above the crash and hiss of the incoming tide, the pounding of a horse's hooves. But before I could investigate, Simon pulled me back into the cave.

'Remember what I said, about not mentioning this, at the house?' he repeated, and when I nodded, he pulled me swiftly into his arms and kissed me.

'That,' he said, when he at last let me go, 'is to remind you to be a good girl and not say a word or give any indication that we are pals, understood?'

I was uncomfortably aware that my face was hot and my pulse leaping. I was sure he could hear my heart pounding. I said, rather coldly, 'It wasn't necessary to do that, in order to help me to keep a secret.'

He grinned. 'Oh, I'm well aware that in other circumstances you might have chastised me for less. That small hand is itching to go into action, isn't it,' and he caught it and held it. 'Go on, smile, m'dear, and admit you didn't loathe it. You'd better, or I'll do it again.'

I was disappointed in him. I must have looked it, because he stopped grinning and the teasing look fled from his eyes. 'Not to worry. Won't do it again,' he promised, letting my hand go. 'Just friends, is that the way you want it?'

I nodded, still unsure of him. He said, 'About the boat trip, weather permitting, we'll make it six a.m. tomorrow, eh? Tide will be right. The weather has a settled look. I'll meet you here.'

It's useless to say that I wasn't thrilled about the prospect as I hurried back along the beach the way I had come. I was thrilled. He had the power to thrill me, and yet I had that lurking doubt that he could turn the charm on at will and had probably charmed

42

other girls just as easily. I wondered why the other secretaries had left, if he was so nice to them. Perhaps, I thought, with a little flutter of apprehension, he had been too nice to them and that was why they had left – or perhaps Lady Isadora had found out, and terminated their service. I wondered fleetingly what she would have to say if she could have seen Simon kissing me inside that cave.

That day was a very heavy day, I remember. Lady Isadora decided to go through the bills outstanding, as well as to get through a normal working day, and just before lunch she decided she would like her desk turned out. 'Sort everything into piles,' she instructed me. 'Quick as you like – the quicker you get it done, the sooner you can clear off to your tea.' She was like that. She boomed directions, in a cheerful manner which made it seem almost but not quite as if she were smiling. 'You'll find a lot of scrap paper we can use, to economise, and there'll be a lot of rubbish. Burn it yourself, in the incinerator in the basement. Someone will show you where.'

Sir Hilton seemed to sense that she had given me extra work because he decided he was in a writing mood and turned out a lot more for me than usual. At this rate, I thought glumly, I would be working half the night. Well, there it was: I needed this job, and it *was* nice, working by the sea. What it would be like in the winter, I didn't pause to think; for a moment, it was rather like a working holiday. I began my turning out with zest.

There really was an awful lot of rubbish. A man brought me a couple of big cardboard boxes, and the first was almost full when for no reason at all my mind wandered and brought back that scene in the caves that morning. I paused to look out of the window at the sea. It was boiling along the edges now; grey, with great white breakers dashing against the shore and sending up flying spray. I remembered thinking fancifully that the sea was trying to blot out the traces of the horse's hooves, and again I felt a shiver of fear as I recalled that black beast thundering right up behind me.

It was then that I recalled that I had heard a horse just before Simon had kissed me. I thought about it. Could it just have been possible that he had kissed me to distract me from investigating as to where the horse was and who was then riding it? But why should he, I thought? At the same time, why should he suddenly kiss me? He hadn't been showing any signs of getting amorous up till then. He had just been showing me a cave ... to keep me from turning my attention to anything going on outside? That, thinking back, was what his manner had suggested. But what could have been going on outside, beyond someone bringing his horse back for him to finish his early morning ride?

It was all very unsatisfactory. It didn't make sense. It was almost as if someone else had been riding that horse, because Simon hadn't seemed aware of the fact that it had come up close behind me and frightened me.

The telephone rang, cutting into my thoughts. It rang too often but I had been led to expect that. Lady Isadora's social life was a wide one, and the arrangements for all her meetings were done by me on the telephone. But they were often distracting.

That particular telephone call took my mind off the incident on the beach that morning, and something else that happened finally drove it clean out of my mind. The piece of paper I held in my hand appeared to be part of a torn letter.

The bit I had read:

...GO ON ANY LONGER, YOU HAVE...

...TOO LONG. IF I DON'T...

...DRED POUNDS BY...

45

I took it over to the window where the light was better, but whichever way I looked at it, it made no different a meaning. There was no signature. It was in neat capitals, with thick black ink. It had been among some old bills (unpaid, of course) and some catalogues of seeds and manures.

Very uneasy, I took it to Lady Isadora. I knew where she was. I could hear her voice raised to someone on the other telephone, in the library. She put the telephone down as I knocked and went in.

She looked surprised to see me. 'Well, what is it?' she asked, in a tone that was hardly promising for what I had to show her. But I was determined to get to the bottom of it, and although I had no doubt that she wouldn't satisfy my curiosity if she didn't feel inclined, at least I could watch her face change, if indeed it was a threatening letter.

Her face changed much more than I expected. 'Where did you find that?' she demanded, almost snatching it from me. But by the time I explained, she had had time to recover herself. She said indignantly, 'It must be some of Sir Hilton's old notes. It can't be of any moment,' and she threw it into the fire. I watched it burn, while she

46

asked me how much more turning out I had to do and I told her.

While I was in there, I thought I would get permission to read some of the books in the library.

'Yes, yes, anything – if you've got time to read,' she said, with the faintest glimmer of a smile. 'I understand you give up your sleep to get your work done.'

I agreed and thanked her. 'I suppose you wouldn't know of a book that tells about the Cave of Gold three or four hundred years ago, would you, ma'am?'

Lady Isadora said, 'No, I wouldn't, or I would have snaffled it myself long ago. And who put that information in your way?'

There was no reason to hide the fact that Mr Rex had, so I told her. I wonder why I didn't tell her that Simon had actually taken me into that cave?

And then she said an odd thing. 'By the way, if you've got the urge to go down to that stretch of beach, watch out for my nephew, Simon – he rides early in the morning. I don't suppose you're likely to be down as early as that, but be careful. He can't see very well since his accident.'

Chapter Three

Of course, he wore dark glasses, I recalled. But he didn't wear dark glasses on the beach. At least, yes, he had had them on when riding that great black horse.

Now I was plunged into doubt. I dare not ask her about the accident. I got out of the library quickly and took the rubbish down to be burned. It would give me time to think.

Tracing back to when I had first seen him, Simon had had no dark glasses on that wet night at the station, when he had shot out to the car. He hadn't behaved like a man with poor sight. On the other hand, when I met him later that same day in the hall, he had dark glasses on but had taken them off to look more closely at me, and he had professed not to have seen me before.

I had seen him several times since then, always with the dark glasses on, but the use of them seemed confined to the house, for when he was leaning against the rock and later took me into the cave, he hadn't had them on. Could it be just possible that there were two of them? That would account for the friendliness of the one and the hostility of the other.

But no, that wouldn't do, because both were called Simon, by staff and family alike. Well, then, if there had been such a bad accident that his sight was impaired, it might just be possible that it had also caused lapses of memory, which might account for him recognizing me at some times and not at others.

I decided to talk to the housekeeper about it. She was always disposed to be friendly with me. I stood down there in the cellars with the damp running down the walls, and I burnt the rubbish in the incinerator, and I thought all round the situation. I had had the feeling at the back of my mind since I had come here, that there was *something* not quite right, and it had seemed to stem from Simon. But I had pushed it into the background. I was determined to make this my life, here in this historic old house, and if there were unexplained things, I had told myself they were no concern of mine, because I had to stay here. I was pledged to myself to make a go of it because I was afraid of the alternative. I dare not look to the future, to the terrible insecurity of it all, with my meagre assets, and I dreaded to look to the past, because I was still reeling from shock.

Funny, how often I had read of people discovering that they didn't belong, that they had been adopted and that it had not been disclosed. Nobody knows what it's like to suddenly discover such a thing. Useless to say it doesn't matter, especially when you're of age; it does matter. The sense of having been cheated is too terrible to consider. And so I stood there, poking the rubbish about until it burnt itself to nothing, and tried not to imagine things that might be happening in this place, to rob me of my new sense of security.

I don't know how long he had been standing there watching me. He merged with the shadows, his face half hidden by the dark glasses. When I realized he was there, I jumped so that the long poker leapt from my hands and fell with a clang on to the stones.

'You startled me! Why didn't you speak?' I said furiously. He wasn't the son of the house just then, so much as a man who had kissed me in a cave and made my pulses leap and race. I had no thought of respect for an employer's relative, so much as anger at someone my own age who had, if only for seconds, found me attractive.

He said, with equal anger, 'I am well aware that resident clerical staff is difficult to come by, but I hardly feel that politeness is too much to ask for, even if respect is practically impossible to expect.'

I left the burning and marched up to him. 'Well, you are the end!' I exploded. 'Quite apart from what you did in the cave, you are quite pleasant to me sometimes, so why do you have to scream at me at other times? I never asked for you to be friends with me but at least don't come the heavy employer just when you feel like it. Things are difficult enough without that!'

I didn't mean to explode like that, and the minute I did it, I stared at him in horror. His face was a study. He took off his glasses and rubbed his eyes, and he said in a very queer voice, 'Would you mind repeating all that, and slowly? I seem to be rather dense today but I confess I wonder if I am going mad or whether you are!'

'I'm sorry,' I muttered. 'I forgot. Lady Isadora only mentioned your accident today. I shouldn't have spoken to you like that.'

'Did she! She had no right to!' he said harshly. 'It's over, forgotten. I'm perfectly all right.'

'Yes, I shouldn't have mentioned it. Oh, let me go and drown myself or something,' I said in exasperation. I seemed to be making *gaffe* after *gaffe,* getting deeper into it with every minute.'

Oddly enough that amused him. He laughed, a queer short little chuckle. 'All right, you didn't know,' he said, and he seemed more like the Simon who had kissed me in the cave. Now I was feeling on safer ground. It must be his accident, of course. So when he urged me to recount every little incident which had annoyed me, in which he had figured, I did so, obligingly, heartily at times.

'Well, let's see, you won't deny almost running me down on that big black horse of yours, now will you – even though you denied it in the cave,' I said rallyingly, as I went back to my burning.

'I went for a ride on Thunder at five thirty this morning, yes,' he said slowly. 'Am I supposed to have almost run you down at that hour?'

'Well, it wasn't much later when you showed me over the cave, was it?' I pointed out. 'Well, about half an hour later, perhaps. Yes, because I came back at six thirty.'

'Do you usually take such early walks? Or

did I make an appointment to meet you there?' He frowned rather anxiously, I thought. 'My aunt tells me I get more forgetful every day but I like to think she exaggerates,' and he sounded just a little apprehensive.

'No, you didn't arrange to meet me,' I said slowly. 'I've seen you around on many occasions since the first day I came and you never appear to recognize me, but that doesn't matter. I'm just staff. But when I ask you if you've seen me, I'd be glad if you'd admit it. You hadn't got your glasses on in the cave, though.'

'I hadn't got my memory with me either,' he said, trying to make light of it but he was obviously worried. 'For I just don't remember going into the damned cave at all. I suppose it was the Cave of Gold.'

'Yes. You were standing at the entrance.' Now I began to feel a bit apprehensive myself. Did he really not remember that he's shown me the cave, arranged to take me in the boat, *kissed me?*

'Come here into the light,' he ordered me. 'What *are* you burning, anyway?'

'Lady Isadora wanted her desk drawers turned out so I did and she wants all this stuff destroyed. Isn't that usual?'

He hesitated. 'It isn't usual for our tame clerical-worker to do anything required of her, let alone burning rubbish down in this dirty hole. Now, turn round to the light.' He took his glasses off and looked earnestly at me. 'What's your name?'

'Carey Constable,' I said, in surprise.

'Age?'

'Now just a minute,' I began, but he frowned, saying, 'You want me to believe I have been told all this. Tell me again. It might come back to me but at the moment I can't recall a thing about you beyond being accosted by you the first evening you came, and told that I'd given you a lift. I hadn't.'

'You remember saying that to me yet you don't remember getting into the Rolls at the station and asking me into the back with you?'

'You sat in the back with me?'

'No, no,' I said impatiently. 'Your chauffeur said something to you and rather pointedly opened his door so I got in beside him. Quite clearly he didn't think I should cadge a lift from the boss, but I didn't know who you were then. It was simply pelting down – the sort of rain that soaks one in a few minutes. I didn't think it was a bad thing to do, to beg a lift in the circumstances.'

'No, of course not,' he said slowly. 'Well, so you are Carey Constable, and I am supposed to have met you on the beach ... how many times?'

'You only saw me, accidentally, on the beach this morning,' I whispered. Now I really was scared.

'Tell me what I said. What I did,' he commanded.

I told him, up to the point when he had kissed me. I couldn't tell him that. I was quite sure he would be very angry to think he had done any such thing.

'So ... I offered to take you in the motor-boat,' he mused. 'Would you mind terribly if I backed out of that invitation? You see, this damned memory of mine ... I can't remember where the boat is, or how to make it go.'

I was suddenly sorry for him. 'It's all right,' I said gently. 'I quite understand. I only wish I'd understood before. And now I must get back to my burning of the rubbish.'

I was acutely embarrassed. I wanted to know more about that accident, but I dare not ask him. He still stood there, frowning a little, and he put his dark glasses on again, and turned to go. But before my very eyes he walked slap into the wall.

I rushed across the stone floor to where he stood recovering. There was a dark smudge on his forehead, that would be a bad bruise pretty soon. 'Whatever–?' I began, but he cut across me.

'Leave me alone! I do those things sometimes. Not to worry. If I stand still, I shall be able to see in a minute. I should have had more patience. That's all.' And he wouldn't let me help him, either. In a few minutes he squared his shoulders and walked quite normally up the steps and out of the place, leaving me, I confess, feeling a little shivery.

When next I had occasion to see the housekeeper, I asked her about his accident.

'Oh, poor Mr Simon, I do feel sorry for him,' she said, at once all cosy and sympathetic. She really was a very nice woman.

'What happened?' I asked again. 'Or is it a secret?'

'Goodness, no, my dear, no secrets in this place, and if anyone says there are, don't you believe them.'

'Oh, I thought there were. The ghostly candles, for instance.'

'Oh, that! That's just a legend. They used to tell the boys in the nursery, so I hear from old Gillett. He's the head gardener. No-one knows how old he is, but he must be over ninety because he was working here, he tells me, when Sir Hilton and Mr Rex were little boys, so it just shows you, doesn't it? It must have been nice here then–'

'But Mr Simon's accident,' I murmured, bringing her back to the point.

'Oh, yes, that. Well, it was rather peculiar, come to think of it, but it was made no secret of. I suppose it could happen. You do hear such strange things. Only yesterday I was reading in the paper–'

'But Mr Simon's accident,' I prompted her again.

'Yes, Mr Simon's accident,' she said, smiling ruefully. 'It was in the Cave of Gold. That dratted cave, I wish they'd block it up. It used to be blocked up all the time when Sir Hilton and Mr Rex were little boys. They'll tell you the story, any day, and I wonder they didn't lose their lives, the little varmints–'

'Mr Simon?' I murmured.

'Yes,' she said, laughing openly now at having diverged so many times. 'Mr Simon. He rides on that black horse of his, you know, very early in the morning. One morning he thought he saw someone go into the cave. It shuts automatically with the tide, they say. There's supposed to be a rocking stone. Me, I wouldn't go near the place.'

'I know. Mr Simon told me about it.'

'Oh, did he? Didn't he tell you what happened to him? What a funny thing! Well, he got off his horse, so they say (I wasn't here then) and went inside to find the person to warn them off, and the rock fell from the ceiling on to his head. He was laid up for a long time. Yes,' she said, thinking.

'Miss Kidby!' I said, bringing her back.

She jumped. 'Yes, well, I shouldn't let on that I've talked about it if I were you, me dear, because between ourselves, the family's a bit worried about him. Has lapses of memory. And there are times, poor fellow, when his sight suddenly goes, just for a while – what were you going to say?'

I had started to say what had happened in the cellars, but then I thought he might not like the people to know he had been down there so long talking to me, so I said instead, 'Isn't there something that can be done for him? With all that money, I should have thought–'

'All what money? The family is very hard up. In fact, there is talk of throwing the Towers open to the public several times a week, and starting the boat trip to see the rocking stone at work. People used to come out here to see it, but the craze fell off. People didn't come here so much when they commercialised Layford. Have you been there, my dear?'

When I unwisely admitted that I hadn't, she started to tell me all about the delights of Layford. I could have kicked myself. I didn't want to know about the lighting that had been turned on by the latest television cutie to get her name known; I didn't want to know how many dance halls there were, nor the size of the fun fair or the number of booths along the front. Miss Kidby obviously liked Layford, or wished to appear to like it so much. I couldn't make up my mind which. I was prepared to believe that she would take the trouble to ride on the double-decker bus into Layford on her day off, and to patronize the Blue Bird Café with its view of the boating pool, and go to the brand new Public Library, but I could hardly imagine her going along the popular end of the promenade to get her photo taken sitting astride a model lion or joining the young folks with a surf board. I let her talk while I thought about Simon Holford, and I couldn't get out of my mind the sight of him that first day when he said, so arrogantly, *I am Holford of Wishborne*. He hadn't seemed the same person.

And the young man fighting his own particular private battle who had talked to me in the cellars, hadn't been the same man who had, with such experience, taken me into his arms to kiss me until my mind should be taken off the sound of the black horse thundering along the edge of the water. I thought round it in bewilderment but all I could think of was that his accident had hurt him mentally giving him two personalities. Ah, but which one did I like so much?

Whatever happened, I should be going for my early morning walk the next day, so I decided to go a little earlier and wait in that cave to see who did ride the black horse.

Before then, however, I had a long session with Sir Hilton, who had decided to double his output per day when he found that there was someone on the premises who didn't mind working hard to get all his notes typed.

While I was sitting in his room waiting for him to find a particular page of notes he had dropped which the breeze had blown under his side of the desk, I said, 'Oh, by the way, Sir Hilton, did you hear about that torn half of a letter?'

He raised his head above the desk. His

face was redder than usual with exertion, though he had refused my offer to poke the sheet of paper out. His eyes were round like marbles and his brows ludicrously raised. He had managed to get his hair disarranged, too, and he looked really comical. But there was nothing comical in his tone as he asked me what letter.

'I thought it was a threatening letter. Well, it sounded like it. Anyway, I showed it to Lady Isadora and she said it was part of your notes and she didn't seem to think you'd want it. She burnt it.'

'Threatening letter?' he thundered. 'What in tarnation are you talking about, girl? What did it say?'

I repeated the gist of it to the best of my recollection and he looked more ludicrous than ever.

'Don't know what you're talking about, girl. Know one thing, though – nothing to do with me, such a letter. Nothing to do with me!'

Chapter Four

It was raining the next day. The sea was an angry mud-grey and it sent the boiling spray flying high. Horse and rider looked like something out of an old tale of the Furies, as they came towards me along the edge of the surf.

I couldn't stop looking at them, they looked so splendid. I cringed back behind a rock as they went by. I don't believe either saw me. I had an old dun coloured raincoat I had found in the garden room and which Gillett said I could borrow, and I had tied a so-called rainproof square over my hair. By that time I must have looked about as damp and unprepossessing as any girl could.

But I had no thought of what I looked like. I raced back to the cave, to be there when he should get there. I had timed it because I had since found out what happened to the horse. It got tethered outside a cottage further along the shore; a cottage in which a one-time servant from the Towers lived, pensioned off.

I waited, and at the time when I thought he should, he arrived – thereby throwing all my anticipation to the winds. I had hoped he would be there before me, so that I could pander to my new suspicion that there were two of them. It was the only thing I could think of.

He had his dark glasses on, and he walked without being too sure of his feet, as well he might, for there was a sharp wind blowing, sending down loose shale from above, and the dry shingle was very unpleasant to walk on.

I said, 'Hello, remember me? Nuisance, who pops up in awkward places and wants to know things.'

'There's no need to fly at me,' he said quite reasonably. 'I came in the hope of stopping any disappointment. Obviously we can't take the boat out today. The sea's too rough.'

'Besides, you can't remember where it is, can you?' I said slowly. Had he forgotten he had said that, too?

Apparently he had, for he asked me what I meant.

'Never mind. I quite understand,' I told him. 'We hadn't better stay here too long, had we? The tide's running in quite quickly.'

'Oh, that's all right,' he said easily. 'Come on in and sit down.'

'But aren't you afraid – I mean, if you can't always see, should you take risks?'

It was only that I cared what happened to him, but manlike, he resented my solicitude. He said coldly, 'You really don't have to be my nursemaid. I suppose you've heard about the accident?'

I drew a deep breath. 'I heard there had been one, but I don't know how it happened. Would you like to tell me about it?'

'No, I wouldn't,' he said. Then he laughed. 'Oh, I'm being a brute, aren't I? Come on in and sit down and let's have a little chat. I know the times of the tides like the back of my hand. I won't take risks, I promise you. Come on,' and he slipped a friendly arm round my shoulder and took me in.

It fascinated me. I had never been to a stretch of coast like this before. It was dry and warm after the chill and the damp outside. His jacket was wet. I said, 'Don't you have a raincoat when you ride that great beast?' and he laughed at me.

'Well, take it off,' I told him, and he did, and draped it over the back of the chair, and I had to let him take mine off, too. He shook it and asked where I'd got it, and he laughed

64

again when I told him.

As he seemed in a relaxed and jolly mood, I ventured to ask him about the rocking stone that closed the cave.

That wiped the amusement from his face. 'Well, they say there was such a thing once, but I've never seen it. Oh, yes, I know that they used to bring the gullible tourists here just before high tide to watch and wait, but I suspect there was something rigged to look like a stone closing it. They didn't get near enough to see, and I don't suppose anyone had the wit to bring field glasses. Well, can *you* see any place where such a thing could be?' and he marched me back to the entrance. I had to admit that there didn't seem to be any such thing, nor any mark in the sand to indicate where it could close.

We talked about such a possibility, and exhausted our fund of ideas, so I asked him about the ghostly candles.

'You are an inquisitive little baggage, aren't you?' He stood leaning easily against the back of the chair, his brown eyes smiling at me, where I sat perched on the chest. He looked like a man very much in command of himself, not at all like the anxious person who had questioned me so closely in the cellars yesterday. 'Well,' he said, in an indulgent tone, 'up in our attics is a branched candle-stick. Somewhere – I can't say for certain just where. It's supposed to appear when there's going to be a death at the Towers.'

'I know. You said all that to me the first night I came, only you assured the chauffeur that it was only someone in the family who would die.'

I waited breathlessly for him to get anxious and ask more about that, but he didn't. He said easily, 'I know I did. He's an old woman. He'd have had us in the ditch or over the cliff edge if I hadn't said that. Now what's the matter?'

'I was only thinking,' I said, rather un-wisely, 'that it's the first time you haven't pretended you'd never given me that lift.'

He looked very oddly at me, then he strolled over to me and took my chin in his hand. 'My love, some poor devil is going to get a nagging wife in you. You keep on and on. Take my advice and don't do it. The male animal doesn't care to be taken up by a smart female.'

'But it's true,' I protested.

'Truth, my dear, is an unpalatable thing, but since we're talking about truth, here is some more of the stuff. A man can say anything he likes, but a wise female won't

66

remind him of it. If she's got any sense, she'll butter him up, make him feel six inches taller than he is, and a devil of a fellow, upright, worthy, and she'll never ever remind him of what poor material he really is.'

'Oh, rot. I'm not the sort of poor-spirited female who would do that! Besides, all men aren't like that! I could never admire a man who couldn't admit he was wrong, for instance. And I would never think much of a man who couldn't bear a female who had as much intelligence as he had!'

He clicked his tongue reprovingly at me. 'You'll learn, my dear, that that is not the way to get the best out of life,' and he bent and kissed me. His kisses took the breath out of me and reduced me to a jelly, but I wasn't really sure that I liked them. Especially after he had told me what he thought of me.

I said so. 'Why *do* you kiss me then?' I demanded.

He laughed again. 'Oh, come now, you're knocking about the world, living out on the job. You must know that a chap likes a girl and kisses but doesn't mean much by it. To be frank, there's a rather engaging air of innocence about you, which rather tends to fight with that slightly hard-boiled manner you have sometimes. I like it.'

'Do you indeed,' I said furiously, feeling let down and angry with myself.

'Yes, and I'll tell you another thing – I like that fighty aspect of you. I've never met a girl who was so ready to fight!'

I got up and shrugged on my damp coat.

'Don't take umbrage because of what I said,' he begged, still amused. 'I wouldn't do you any harm. You must know that. Not worth it, considering you're working in the house, and everyone's darling because you apparently don't mind how much of a doormat they all make you!'

I tied the head scarf round and under my chin, catching the skin in the knot as I did so, but I hardly noticed, I was so angry. I marched out of the cave. He strolled after me, and if the thought occurred to me that he ought to get out of there and up to the house where he would be safe, before it was high tide, I wasn't going to say so, I was so livid. Besides he'd probably give me a set-down for my pains if I did.

I marched back along the sands, un-conscious that the rain had almost stopped, unconscious of the beauty of the grey morning, the watery sun peeping through the mist to make a white water line from horizon to shore. I saw nothing, only myself, made to look a fool about a man I was beginning to care for, but who was just playing about with me – one of the staff, who would probably follow the others before long. Perhaps that's why the other typists hadn't stayed: not because of Lady Isadora sending them packing but because they were tired of Simon playing about with their affections.

I worked harder than ever, and kept out of his way, so I didn't see him for two days. I heard his voice, occasionally, and I must say it didn't sound amused or cocksure as it had in the cave. My heart ached, but I gave myself a good talking to and tried to forget about him, and for my early morning walks I took the other direction, through the sleeping village and up to the hills. It wasn't as beautiful or as interesting, but at least I didn't have to see him on that black horse, or run the risk of having my heart torn out of me by one or the other of his interesting approaches. I couldn't decide which was the more perfidious: the frank and open philanderer in the cave, or the anxious half blind young man with the faulty memory, shyly making my acquaintance in the cellars. Either was a pretty deadly mixture and I decided I wanted none of it.

I don't know what would have happened if Lady Isadora's maid hadn't made a fuss about me working late in my room. She was elderly, not so much of a luxury as an almost pensioned servant. She had been Lady Isadora's mother's maid, and now she generally made herself useful in any way that was required of her and within her limits. She had rheumatism, slept badly, but was devoted and easily hurt. Poor old Winnie Fenning, I wonder at this distance whether she ever realised that it was her complaining of the tapping of my typewriter keeping her awake, that might well have sparked off everything that happened then.

She complained and, pampered as she was, she had her way. Lady Isadora said that she appreciated my devotion to duty but if that was the way I was going to conduct my working life, then it must be down in the library, and not in my bedroom, waking the other staff.

I brought the portable typewriter down, with resignation. It was a long way down; three pairs of back stairs, mostly unlighted. Then I had to go up again and fetch down the trays of files and papers for each person.

The library was a large room, shadowy, its

70

walls lined with books, its ceiling propped by thick stone pillars. The main lights were off. I worked in a small pool from one desk lamp and it was shivery, after the cosiness of my warm, light little bedroom. The woodwork of floors and book shelves creaked and groaned in the silence after the house had retired to sleep. Several times I started up out of my seat, then, laughing at my fears, sat down again and forced myself to become interested in my work to the exclusion of everything else.

One thing about Wishbourne Towers bothered me; there were no pets. Not a dog or a cat about anywhere. Remembering that, my flesh began to creep as I heard a small noise outside.

I put out the lamp, and using a small pocket torch I got to the door in safety, but once there, I couldn't open it. I called myself a coward and anything else I could think of, but I kept thinking, not so much of that silly story of the candles, but of the likelihood that someone was trying to burgle the castle. There was a lot of solid silver around which might well attract a marauder. I cursed myself for not having the wit to go to bed like the rest of the staff, in the safety of the upper floor, rather than to stay down here, all alone in the small hours.

Sickened at such thoughts, I gritted my teeth, put out my torch and wrenched the door open.

Outside the door was the main hall. In common with such houses, there was a great yawning open fireplace, now never used but filled with a huge urn of flowers. On the walls were circular shields and behind them criss-crossed, ancient weapons – spears and halyards. A solitary suit of armour stood against the wall, and on this a ghostly light played, from something on the table in the middle of the hall. A branched candelabra, lit, but transparent, through which I could see the suit of armour.

I don't think I had ever felt so ill in my life. I leaned weakly against the lintel of the door, and the scream I heard was torn from my own throat. The noise of that scream echoed and echoed all over the house and soon doors were beginning to open and voices and footsteps could be heard. I recall that Lady Isadora was well to the fore, as one would expect, but of course, by the time she arrived at where I was standing, there was nothing. Only the moonlight filtering through the high windows above the door, and the feeble beam of my own small torch.

I heard my own voice saying, over and over again, 'I saw The Candles! The Wishbourne Candles!'

Sir Hilton said, 'Rot, girl! Where did you see them?' and when I told him, showed him the exact spot, he was silenced.

Mr Rex said, 'Well, I suppose it could have been someone fooling about, lighting the originals, and removing them?' but he didn't sound very convinced, nor was he when I roundly said, 'I could see that suit of armour right through them. They were transparent.'

One of the girls from the village, a new one, had hysterics. Funny, people don't seem to have them nowadays, but she did, and the housekeeper smartly smacked her face and she stopped her noise. But everyone looked pretty sick. All the lights were put on. I looked round for Simon, and he was looking at me very oddly, then he polished his dark glasses and put them on, and he didn't speak to me. He just kept looking across the intervening space at me.

Lady Isadora questioned me, then ordered tea to be made for everyone, allowing that it was a shock to be roused. Then everyone was sent back to bed, including myself. My work had to be left, but to be honest I had no more heart for it.

Neither had I, next morning, when it was found that the chauffeur wasn't in his room. He was later found in a huddled position on the back stairs, dead.

Chapter Five

Well, that was what I gathered, that he was dead. There was a blanket right up to his face as he was taken by on a stretcher. And then I heard later that he wasn't quite dead, just in a very bad way. Everyone was in such a flap that night, I am quite prepared to believe that only the ambulance men would have known for certain what state he was in. 'I've never seen a dead person before. How do you know they're dead?' the maid who had hysterics quavered, as she tried to sweep up the fireplace in the library next morning.

'I think you'd know,' I said shortly, 'although I haven't seen a dead person, either. Don't worry, they'll take very good care of Mr Logsden, I'm sure.'

'I hope so, miss,' she sobbed. 'He was very kind to me. Me not having no father, I mean. Never shouted at me when I broke things, not like Miss Kidby.'

I was surprised. I would have thought she would like Miss Kidby better. The house-keeper had certainly been more friendly to me than the chauffeur, who had looked down his nose at me that first night, and hadn't liked Simon giving me a lift at all. I shivered. The chauffeur had been so frightened, inordinately frightened, it seemed to me; a grown man caring about a silly legend! Yet there it was; the ghostly candles had been seen and the chauffeur had died.

In the cold light of day I thought about it and asked myself if I had really seen right through those candles. Surely it had been a trick on someone's part. The thing was to find the candles and their candelabra, and see if they were dusty, cobwebby. If they were clean, the chances were that they had been lit and whipped away when we weren't looking. It must have been a parlour trick. I couldn't have seen something supernatural. I just wouldn't believe it.

But if it had been a parlour trick, besides being in very bad taste, it had also been very slickly done, because of the time factor.

The maid finished her job at the fireplace. Six o'clock struck, and I suddenly wanted fresh air. I decided to take my walk. She said, still standing there, 'Miss, did you really see a ghost? I mean, *was* it a ghost, like, or were you having everyone on?'

I turned sharply and looked at her. 'What

76

do you mean by that?'

She looked decidedly unhappy about it, but she was dogged. 'Begging your pardon, miss, my mum says there's no such thing as a ghost, and she'd give me a lambasting if she was to hear of this. And you being seen with Mr Simon, who's up to his tricks – leastways, he used to be before he had his accident – and, well, if it hadn't been for poor Mr Logsden copping it on the back stairs, I might have thought you and Mr Simon had done it between you, just for a lark.'

There was only one thing in all that tirade that seriously bothered me just then, and that was the thought that we had been seen, Simon and I together. 'How do you know – I mean, what makes you say Mr Simon and I have been seen? Where? Who?'

'My young brother goes shrimping early in the mornings, and he likes to see Mr Simon ride, and he said he saw you and Mr Simon go into the Cave of Gold.'

I sighed. I ought to have known. In a small place like this where everyone knew everyone else, what else could I have expected? I decided to be open about it, as far as I could.

'I walk on the shore. I was looking for the Cave of Gold. He offered to show me.

77

That's all.'

She looked unconvinced. I supposed that her young brother had seen us both times. Perhaps she had had occasion to go to the cellars when I had been burning the rubbish. I said, 'All right, better pop off if you don't want the housekeeper to be on your tail,' so she took the hint and went. But she hadn't been satisfied.

Logsden was alive when he reached hospital, but only just. He died later. The family were clearly upset about it. They had a conference, and didn't give me any work to do. I had a good chance to pull up, with great pleasure, because my walk that morning had been unrewarded. Simon didn't take his horse out, nor was he at the cave. The beach was deserted, and it was difficult to believe that I had been kissed in that fold in the cliffs, nor that any other of the things had happened to me since I had come here.

The next day there was more trouble. We were in the newspapers. Well, we expected to be in the local newspapers because of the inquest. The local police had visited the scene and been very courteous. Lady Isadora was well known locally and respected. They had to do their job but clearly it was only routine. Logsden had heard a noise, come downstairs to investigate, slipped and hit his head a blow that had cost him his life. It was as simple as that. The inquest was routine, too. Accidental death. But before that, we had the Press to cope with.

Not just the little paragraph in the nationals about a servant falling to his death after a ghost scare, but the work of an enterprising reporter who had been sent down from London on some other job which had turned out to be a damp squib and who had been determined to get something out of it.

I heard Lady Isadora talking on the telephone. 'He says his name is Percy Drewett and that he's been to you already for a story.'

That would be to Four Winds, where there had been a burglary, I thought. Checking on Mr Drewett's credentials.

'Late thinking, I'm afraid,' Lady Isadora went on. 'He said he needed just another story to add to a series and if it comes off it'll mean big money for us. Yes, well, my brothers are all for it, as you imagine. All right, my dear, if you say he's all right, then he can have carte blanche and we may not expect him to make off with the silver.'

So Percy Drewett came to Wishbourne and made friends with everyone. Heaven knew what he got out of us by way of a story. I was only conscious of trying to hold things back and finding myself confiding in him as if I had known him all my life. He was that sort of young man. And when he wanted to see the original candelabra, I was, of course, the unfortunate person who had to take him up to the attics. 'It's no use, you know,' I told him. 'I'm new here myself. I can't think why the housekeeper didn't bring you up.'

He grinned unrepentantly. 'She doesn't know about it. She isn't being very co-operative, you know. Something to do with Master Simon.' He said it as if he thought it was rather funny.

'What about him?' I asked sharply.

'I was laughing at the old dear herself, not that arrogant young brute who, I gather, is the sole heir of the Holfords.'

'What about him?' I asked remorselessly. But of course, it merely betrayed to him that Simon was rather special to me, although sometimes I felt I could have cheerfully murdered him.

'The fact is,' Percy Drewett said, as he toiled after me, up the spiral staircase which was the last stage of the journey to the attics, 'there's a maid who thinks you and Simon were having an elaborate joke on

80

anyone who cared to fall for it. Were you?'

'I wasn't. I can't vouch for anyone else,' I said shortly.

'I merely mentioned it,' he said conversationally, 'because if it was only a joke, then there's no lovely lolly in it for your bosses, and I gather they do need a lot of the ready, to settle some pretty pressing bills of staggering proportions.'

'How did you – I mean, what made you think that?' I gasped.

'Oh, come *on,*' he chided. 'We press bods are a low lot, when it comes to gathering information. Slip a note here and there, and there's no telling what you find out. And I've found out your arrogant family here are pretty empty in the pockets.'

I loathed him. I loathed myself for bringing him up here. Much good might it have done me, for he would have come himself. Lady Isadora had admitted to her friends that she wanted the cash. As if nobody knew it already!

We went into the attics. Other people might call the attics the space under the roof and feel pretty pleased with themselves if they can get a room fixed up in it, big enough to swing a cat. The attics at Wishbourne could have been turned into a ballroom triple the size of the one downstairs, if the roof hadn't been so low. They were vast. 'Like to search for the candelabra yourself?' I mocked at him, as he eyes came out on stalks.

He gave a swift and comprehensive look around. It was clear that the attics weren't allowed to degenerate too much. Most of the things up here were items of furniture and ornaments that had been temporarily removed from the less important rooms, and they were covered with dust sheets. There was the usual dressmaker's dummy, and a couple of hand-sewing-machines, a birdcage and some cleaning gear; sundry old-fashioned trunks and chests, brought up the other stairs at the far end, because the spiral staircase would have been too awkward. Lamps and heaters by the dozen, extra chairs for parties, boxes of party decorations and extra pots and glasses in their boxes. I shouldn't have been surprised if Miss Kidby hadn't kept all these entered in her little book, so that she knew where to put her hands on anything.

But there was no need to worry about the candelabra. It was hanging close to the ceiling. A tall man could have handed it down on the instant. But no tall man had touched it for years. It was the one thing that was festooned with cobwebs and the dust of ages, as if even Miss Kidby was reluctant to clean it.

'Well, that's that, isn't it, love?' Percy grinned. 'It really does look as if it is a case of the good old supernatural. Your bosses are in the money, but me, I shouldn't care to stay in this house.'

'You mean you believe in such things?' I couldn't understand it, he looked a hard-bitten young man if ever there was one.

He stood making notes, and drawing a good if rough sketch of the thing. 'I suppose I should say I do, having slept in several haunted houses for the purpose of my series.'

'You mean you've actually seen a ghost?' I asked him.

He laughed. 'What a daft question, from you! I thought you were an intelligent girl. Well, let's put it this way. I've slept through – or tried to sleep – through a night in one of these places, and I didn't see someone in a white sheet, if that's what you mean. But I did,' he said, fixing me with very thoughtful eyes, 'see *something*, heaven knows what, and I'm not prepared to say it was rigged, because,' and he took his eyes off me and went on with his sketch, 'there was a very strong sensation of nastiness in the atmosphere. Evil if you like. And you may quote me. There!'

My heart started to hammer. There was logic in what he said. But honestly I couldn't say that I had felt any such thing. I could only say, since he looked expectantly at me and clearly expected me to offer my contribution to the conversation, 'I saw right *through* them.'

As he didn't answer, I went on, 'Nobody could have taken them away – if it had been rigged, I mean – because I was looking at them all the time.'

'You mean they suddenly vanished, and all went dark? Or that they floated away?' he asked me, quite seriously.

That was when I made the discovery that I hadn't seen the going of the candles. The maid had gone into hysterics and the housekeeper had slapped her face, and while I had been looking up the stairs at this, I had been conscious that the hazy light had gone, and the candles were no longer there.

In my heart I thought it was a parlour trick but I just couldn't see how it had been done, and besides, the originals hadn't been touched. Could it be that there was another branched candelabra that had been used? Painted with phosphorus paint, perhaps?

'No,' I found myself saying, 'it must have been an apparition, though I still can't believe it. I hope I don't see it again, but there was the story that if a Holford gave someone a lift and the candles were seen, someone would die, and it came true.'

'Oh, yes, the chauffeur. He started to say something. I was there,' the reporter said.

'What did he say?' I gasped.

'What would you expect to hear that he'd said?' Percy Drewett asked, in a mild tone that almost deceived me.

'How he met his death, of course,' I said at once.

'Well, he didn't, and I really do think I should report to one of your bosses what he confided in me. Perhaps you'd take me to them?'

'No need for that. One is here,' Simon's voice said. His brown eyes regarded the reporter with hostility. 'What did the chauffeur say?'

He was in a rough guernsey with a high neck and it wasn't very clean, as if he had rubbed up against somewhere, and his slacks were extremely casual for that normally well-tailored young man. And in me rose the hostility that appeared sometimes when with him, and which I couldn't account for. I only knew at this moment that I didn't like him at all. Here was the enemy, and I flinched from him.

Percy was in no way put out. 'Well, you'll do,' he said pleasantly. 'The chauffeur was trying to tell me something about the lift that was given to the young lady here,' and he looked at me. 'The chappie seemed to feel let down. He said Mr Simon had promised him that the threat of death only applied to members of the Holford family. Not to the staff.'

Chapter Six

Simon laughed, a not very friendly laugh. 'Of course I did,' he said. 'Was it likely I'd alarm him more? He was shaking like a jelly, and it was such a lot of rot. Me, I don't believe in ghosts.'

'Yet he died,' Percy said.

'If he couldn't pick his feet up when going downstairs, whose fault is that?' he asked easily.

'True,' Percy allowed. 'Yet you saw the Candles, sir?' His politeness was very persuasive, and Simon fell for it.

'No, I didn't, if you must know. But I heard a lot about it. If you want to know, the only one who appears to have seen them is young Carey here, and if you ask me, she'd fallen asleep over her typewriter, dreaming of ghostly candles, probably, and thought she saw them.'

I stood shaking my head. 'The others all came running.'

'Yes, when you screamed,' he said. 'You set up such a row, what else did you expect?'

'I'd like to see it myself. Do you think you could give someone else a lift?' Percy Drewett asked Simon.

'I don't mind, but how will you know when it will happen again? According to our newest secretarial treasure, it didn't happen on the day I was daft enough to give her a lift, but waited for a week or so. Or do you propose to board on us all that time?'

'Why not?' the reporter said blandly. 'My paper allows me expenses. Lady Isadora said I could stay if I wished. Yes, it might be a good idea.'

'Well, it wouldn't,' Simon said, flatly. 'I don't want a lot of reporters to breakfast–'

'Only one,' Percy said meekly.

'You sure?' Simon asked suspiciously.

'Don't you think I can do the job on my own ... sir?' Percy said just a trifle mockingly.

Simon flushed angrily, and said something about if his aunt saw any money and publicity out of this, he'd be very much surprised, and he strode off and left us.

'Now, what are you looking so upset about?' Percy asked me.

I looked up into his face, a nice, ordinary, open face for a young man; rather tough about the jaw, but none of Simon's good looks or the aristocratic set of his mouth. Nothing like that for Percy; he was just a young man on a job, a young man scenting more in it than anybody was willing to give away.

I said, rather uncomfortably, 'The house-keeper should have brought you up here. Simon shouldn't have come. I can't think why he did.'

'Or why he changed or how he got dirty?' Percy didn't miss much. 'What's the matter with you, Carey Constable?' he demanded.

'I should have warned you. He's had an accident. They say a rock fell on him in a local cave, and it's affected his sight and his memory. Sometimes he thinks he hasn't said or done something, sometimes he doesn't recognize people. It might cloud the issue, you know.'

'It might indeed,' Percy said, with a great deal of interest. 'Tell me more.'

'There isn't any more to tell really,' I said. 'Except–'

'Go on,' he encouraged.

'I don't know whether I should mention this, but Simon didn't really remember giving me that lift or saying those things to the chauffeur.'

Percy didn't say much to that. I wondered

what he thought and whether I had done the wrong thing in mentioning it. I couldn't have said why I did, or why I felt it was necessary to mention it. Merely because Simon sometimes gave me the impression that he honestly hadn't said the things that I had heard him say.

Of course, the press weren't going to wait about indefinitely for the ghost to oblige. They wanted the thing set up, so Simon, smiling grimly, said he'd go and find someone to give a lift to.

I thought at first that he was joking. I saw him the next morning on that black horse. It was a peerless morning. I could see him coming in the distance. I was almost at the cave. I decided I would go along to the cottage to meet him, but of course, I couldn't get there in time. I climbed up where I could see the cottage in the distance. Horse and rider stopped there, and an old man ran out. A little shrivelled person, bent but still spry. I couldn't see him clearly enough to discern his features, only his shape. Wild grey hair sticking up, tall sea boots, dark trousers and guernsey which came up to his chin. A typical fisherman type. I wondered what he had done by way of service up at Wishbourne before they had pensioned him. Simon didn't dismount from his horse; he merely leaned down and said something, and then turned and went on. I watched him along the shore until he turned sharply and rode inland.

Disappointed, I went down again to the level of the cave. He wouldn't be coming this morning, then. I sat on a rock to think. Wasn't I an idiot, falling in love with a man I loathed sometimes?

I don't know how long I had sat there, but suddenly hands came on me from behind and he was there, pulling me to my feet, into his arms, and kissing me silly. I had no time to be alarmed because of the swiftness of his action, but afterwards I wondered a little. It was so odd. I hadn't heard the horse's hooves. I didn't know where he had left the horse. Perhaps he had just ridden a little way and come back. I didn't know. I only knew, with a rising sense of bewilderment, that his kisses only made me excited, not pleasurably so. I was aware that when he kissed me I had no will to be critical of him, and yet there were so many things I wanted to ask him.

At last he let me go. 'All right,' he plunged right in to tell me, 'I know what you're thinking. You didn't hear me arrive. You don't like the clothes I'm wearing. You loathe me at times. All right, let's take all that as read, and tell me what the aunt and uncles say when you're in there with them and I can't get in.'

'Say?' I asked, bewildered by his swift verbal attack. 'About what?'

'Oh, don't be silly,' he said impatiently. 'About the press stunt and the money and everything.'

'They say they'll be glad to receive some money but it isn't certain yet that they will. There's got to be proof.'

He laughed. 'Well, we can't really wait for the old Candles to oblige, can we? We shall have to make them perform.'

'Make them?' I asked, not quite sure what he was getting at. 'You mean that last performance *was* a hoax on your part?'

'I didn't say that,' he snapped. 'I said we shall have to make a performance in the future.'

'Well, if you can, I suppose.' I was suddenly more doubtful than I had ever been before. 'Can you?'

'I don't know. I've seen it done. Sometimes it's done with mirrors and sometimes with a moving camera. The great thing is to be slick with timing.' He looked fretted, worried.

I said, 'I may be old-fashioned, but I don't

like it, and I would appreciate it if you told me how it was done last time. I mean, if it was only a trick, I should feel better about it because I happened to be working down-stairs alone and it wasn't very nice.'

I had caught his attention. 'Yes, I meant to ask you about that,' he said. '*Why* were you downstairs alone? Surely you work in your bedroom at night?'

There it was again. Just as if he were an-other person, not in the place, unaware of what arrangements had been made. I said carefully, because I didn't want to upset him, 'Lady Isadora's maid complained of the tapping of my typewriter.'

'Oh, was that it? That old – oh, well, poor old Winnie Fenning, she's been a faithful servant. I suppose they *would* give way to her.'

Everything in me wanted to scream out: 'But you were there at the time! You heard it discussed! You said a few things about it!' But I couldn't. It broke my heart to see the confused, bothered look in his eyes when he was caught out not remembering.

He absently kneaded the back of my neck with his right hand. It sent sparks all over me, yet I wasn't happy. I wanted to have it out with him, ask him what it was all about.

But it was no use. He was, at the moment, like a man on fire with an idea. He said, after some thought, 'We must help poor old Aunt Isadora to get some cash. It's no fun trying to run that great barn of a place.'

'Why don't you all sell out and go into a smaller house?' I asked, without thinking. My own sense should have told me they wouldn't be able to bring themselves to do that.

'Because, my angel, we are an old family, and our roots are here,' he said. He didn't say it gently, explaining to someone who hadn't had that problem before. He said it harshly, scornfully, as if I ought to have known what he felt, and that I was an abysmal simpleton not to understand. I flushed, acutely miserable to have fallen so low in his eyes.

'I'm sorry,' I said. 'But to me that seems logical, or better still, to have the public pay to come in and see–'

'No!' It was almost a shout. 'I hate strangers,' he said, rubbing his forehead. Then his old gay mood was back again and he laughed. 'You must think I'm a peculiar fellow, but the fact is, my lamb, my ancestors really did come over with the Conqueror, and there aren't many of us left. We loathe to

94

be stared at.'

'Then what *will* you do?' To me there was no answer to that, but he had one.

'We will make the old Candles perform, which will set up a hoo-hah which will be perfectly proper, and people will come to stare from the outside, and only the experts will come to the inside. Oh, I see them all, the exorcizing gentry and the professors, all looking very wise and taking measurements and listening at the walls, and the press won't offer us chickenfeed, they will pay us in thousands to have the privilege of taking little pictures for people to prop up on their breakfast tables and shiver over, and envy us perhaps for being such an old family ... and we shall find the gold.'

The last few words were said in a whisper, a fanatical whisper that made me shiver.

I felt impelled to say, 'But won't you have an awful lot of tax to pay on it?'

He decided to make it a joke. 'I like to say that, my lamb, because I always get a different comment. Every time! It's so entertaining. But no-one has ever asked me about tax before. Tell me, what was your father's job? Did he have a lot of money?'

'I don't know. I don't even know who my father was,' I said. Withdrawn as always, I didn't want to discuss it at this moment, because it was too sharp a comparison. He came from an old, old family and I came from heaven knew where, an unknown without even a name I could call my own. I said, trying him out for size, 'I was adopted.'

Distaste showed in his face, as I believe I had known it would. I moved out of his arms and he let me go. He looked round him, at the walls of the cave, and at the great line of cliffs, and dissatisfaction turned his mouth down. 'The Cave of Gold! Damned silly name, isn't it? And this isn't where the gold will be either. Oh, don't ask me where – I've got a theory and I'll put it to the test, but it isn't here. This is just the showpiece. All for publicity. Swindle, really, because there isn't a rocking stone, either. That was set around as a rumour, and you've no idea how a rumour takes on, in this place. Of course, the villagers know better. Fisherfolk, know every inch of the coastline. But they know which side their bread's buttered – I'm willing to place a bet on it that old Jimmy Noy could get a clean fiver from a load of tourists if he liked to tell the tale. What he'd seen on the way to the village this morning, he'd start.'

He stood there laughing to himself, almost

as if I weren't there.

'Who's Jimmy Noy?' I asked him.

He looked up, frowning at me. 'The old boy in the cottage – where the horse is tethered.'

'It isn't tethered there. It's elsewhere,' I couldn't stop myself saying.

He looked at me almost with loathing. I said quickly, 'Come up and look – you can see the cottage from here.'

He followed me, climbing silently behind me. But when he reached there, I could see the black horse, tethered to the gate as usual. 'Sorry, it wasn't there just now,' I said.

He didn't answer. He just looked consideringly at me. A look I didn't much like.

'Simon,' I burst out, 'why are you cross with me today? You weren't like this before!'

He climbed down in silence to the cave mouth and waited for me. 'I've had an accident, remember? Not really reliable. You have to make allowances for me,' he said harshly, yet a gleam of amusement in his eyes.

I took it that he was recovering his good humour, so I asked him something I had wanted to for a long time. 'I know, Simon, and you ought to wear your dark glasses –

the light here is very bright. Where is the scar?'

'Scar?' he whispered, his amusement gone in a flash.

'Yes, on your head. When the rock hit you,' I said.

He stared at me, so long that I flushed uncomfortably. I said, 'Oh, sorry, I am a tactless thing. I shouldn't have mentioned it. Forgive?' I said quickly. 'Only you did mention the accident first.'

'We'd better both forget about it,' he said tersely.

I started to go. He said, 'Where are you off to?'

'You don't want me here. I'd better go anyway.'

He pulled me back. 'You stay here till I tell you to go,' he said sharply. Then, as I looked surprised, he laughed, and started to kiss me again.

'Don't! I wish you wouldn't. Not in this mood,' I pleaded. 'I like it when you're in a nice mood, but you're hating everyone this morning.'

'That's your fault,' he said, fondling my face, running his hands up through my hair, kissing my eyelids. 'Why do you come here first thing in the morning?'

'But you know that, Simon. I must have fresh air and exercise, and it's no good leaving it until the family gets up. They all want their work done at once. There's no time to breathe.'

'Who showed you how to get out?' he said, and when I told him, again in some surprise, he frowned, as if angry with himself for not remembering. 'Well,' he said, 'just don't let Lady Isadora know, that's all. She hates people to be wandering around before she's up.'

'The staff do, and I'm staff,' I reminded him.

Again he was angry. 'Don't say that! Oh, well, what's the use? Well, if you're staff, do as you're told and tell me what the uncles talk about when you're shut in with them, taking notes? Do they ever discuss how to find the gold?'

'Oh, Simon,' I said, laughing helplessly, 'I told you before, they don't discuss it. I did ask once if they thought there was any, and they treated it as rather a joke. Well, as a legend, and it was funny if anyone treated it seriously. You know the kind of thing.'

'Well, I don't. It's there, somewhere. Can you promise me they haven't any interest in trying to find it?'

'No, I can't, because for all I know, they may wait until I'm out of the room before they discuss it. It would be private and personal, wouldn't it, the same as it is with you? Well, you never tell me what your theory is, do you?'

'No, because I don't want you talking to someone else about it.'

'Who would I talk to about it?'

'Oh, I don't mean *knowingly,*' he said.

I wasn't listening very hard at the time. I was watching his eyes. Today they didn't look odd, as they had done in the cellar. It was hard to say just how odd they had looked. I couldn't have explained; just odd, like eyes that would lose their sight on the instant, as they did.

Thinking of that incident, I said to him, 'Simon, has it happened since, you know what I mean? What happened in the cellars?'

He looked perfectly blankly at me. He quite clearly had no idea what *had* happened in the cellars. And as he was staring at me, trying to fathom my meaning, we heard horses' hooves. He looked round in a frustrated sort of way, as the black horse tore by, down by the water's edge, and though I couldn't swear to it at that distance, it seemed to me that the young man riding it wore dark glasses.

Chapter Seven

I watched it out of sight, then I turned fearfully to him. 'So there *are* two of you! Are you twins?'

He looked blankly at me, but his powers of pulling himself together were quite remarkable.

He said irritably, 'Twins, no! Don't be an idiot, Carey! What is more to the point is, who the devil is riding my horse?' and he left me, to hurry back to the cottage, presumably to find out what was going on.

His remark made everything normal. I was an idiot to have thought there were two of them. Of course it must have been someone else riding that black horse. He'd give that person hell, I thought, in appreciation.

I know I had said I ought to be getting back to the house, but somehow I wanted to wait, and see what he had found out. I supposed it would be natural of some young local man, seeing the horse tethered there, to want to try it out. But I wanted to know. I wanted to see him again, especially now he had categorically denied that he was a twin. Now I could be assured whenever I saw him, that if he didn't appear to be the same as last time, it was only because of his accident. And I would have to remember not to mention it to him again. Of *course* he would be too touchy to speak of it!

So I went up the passage into the big chamber of the cave, and sat down to wait for him. I thought over all that he had said, and it was while I was waiting that I made a rather odd discovery. I suppose it was the crumbs on the floor that started it.

A lot of crumbs, near the table, and near the oak chest. Normally I suppose I wouldn't have taken much notice. I might have thought that picnickers had been here, yet I seemed to remember that it hadn't been like that when I came here before.

Well, I was in an inquisitive mood, I suppose. I got up and opened the chest. I had sat on it before now. Indeed, Simon had invited me to sit on it while he used a chair at the table. I should have been surprised if I could have looked inside it first.

It was completely filled with food and the means to cook it. Tinned goods, wrapped bread, milk; a primus stove and some oil, matches, a torch and spare batteries. Everything, in fact, for someone to make a base here.

I closed the lid in bewilderment, and poked around further but I couldn't find any sleeping arrangements. Simon here all day? Looking for that gold he was certain would be there, somewhere? Then where did he sleep? Well, of course, he slept at Wishbourne, but how could he get there, once the tide was in, or the light had faded from the day?

He returned before I had time for any more brilliant deductions and such was his new manner, that I managed to restrain myself from mentioning my find. I said instead, 'I waited for you. I thought you might want to tell me more about your idea for getting the Candles to work.'

He said sourly, 'Not now, Carey, not now. There's a chap staying with old Noy. Infernal cheek, riding off on Thunder like that. I gave him a piece of my mind.'

'Oh, so that's what happened,' I said, and I sounded relieved. I know I did. And he flashed me a rather penetrating glance. Altogether I thought it might be as well if I returned to Wishbourne without delay.

'Are you going to walk back with me?' I asked, and received another odd look from him.

'No,' he said, 'having got Thunder back, I shall ride in the back way. You'd better get going, Carey. On the whole, I don't think you'd better risk setting my aunt's back up, being seen walking with me.'

So that was it! Well, it was sense. I departed quite satisfied, and he noticed it and seemed easier, I think now, looking back. But at the time I worried all the way back about the changeableness of his disposition, and how it would all end. Well, of course, I told myself, if I had any sense, I would know how it would end. Where was the sense, I berated myself, of falling in love with a man like him, who would never dream of marrying his family's stenographer, especially one who didn't know who she was!

I was so depressed I didn't care what happened. All I really was glad about was that I had been right, and there weren't two of them. Twins would have been the end. I would never have known which one I was talking to. But there was this to fret over: if he wasn't a twin he was going to be a very tricky person to get on with, after that accident!

I decided to find out more about it. It might be a good idea to ask everyone. Weave it into general remarks and see what I got by way of offered information.

I started that day on Lady Isadora. 'Mr Simon rides that big black horse every morning,' I remarked. 'I suppose that accident is far enough back in the past for him to be all right on that brute.'

I was opening the mail at the time. Usually I paid great attention; unmarked letters to me, those marked private or personal I flipped over into the pile facing her. We had a sort of unspoken bet on, who would get them opened and read first. I was so busy plotting to get information about Simon's accident that I didn't notice what I was opening. It was marked strictly personal and the missive was in block capitals, unsigned.

Lady Isadora, preoccupied on her side of the desk said, 'What? No, always worrying about it but who listens to me? He's not long been out of hospital. What do you expect, with a rock that size hitting him? It's a wonder he's alive to tell the tale.'

I sat staring stupidly at the missive in my hands, wondering what I should do about it. It read: IF YOU HAVEN'T THE SENSE TO LEAVE THE CASH IN THE REQUIRED PLACE I WILL HAVE TO COME AND GET IT IN PERSON ... TODAY.

She said, 'What's that you've got there, Carey?' so without a word I passed it over.

You wouldn't have been able to tell whether she was upset or not, by her colour. It didn't change, but she did go very still, and her hands shook a little.

I said, 'I'm sorry. It's talking. Didn't notice what I was opening. Afraid I read it.'

'That's all right,' she said. 'So now you know.'

'The same person who wrote the letter you thought belonged to Sir Hilton's notes?' I suggested gently, and her mouth slipped briefly into a rueful smile.

'The same,' she agreed.

'Will I get the police?' I asked, very quietly.

She said, in the same quiet tone, 'You will not. At least we have the doubtful advantage of its being a secret, which it won't be if you get the police in.'

So, having offered my one bright idea and had it summarily rejected, I just sat there, looking at her.

She said, 'You seem to have become one of the family. I don't know what Simon's intentions are, but I feel that I can tell you, without having to wonder if you'll take off next week and leave us in the lurch. I am, of course, being threatened about money. Nine hundred pounds.'

I did her the justice of not squeaking to

the ceiling about such a sum but I felt like it. Because I knew that her unpaid bills were in the plural and this was just one of them. How many other people were threatening her, I couldn't think.

She went on, in that level tone, 'I was hoping to pull off the story of the Candles, so that the press would pay us the rather gorgeous sum they promised.'

I nodded. 'Well, they're going to, aren't they?'

She looked at me. 'Is that what Percy told you? For a plain unexceptional little thing you do attract the other sex, don't you? My brothers won't hear a word said against you, either.'

I went pink. That was a back-handed compliment, if ever there was one. I said hastily, 'Oh, it's only because there's a shortage of young women here, ma'am.' But she merely raised her eyebrows.

After some thought, she murmured, 'I really think we must put on a show for the press. The Candles won't come to us so we must go to them. And we must see the press boys are there on time, and what is much more important, someone must see that their cameras won't be rolling because we mustn't allow the Candles to be filmed.

That would be disastrous.'

I must have shown dismay in my face, at the thought of her *and* Simon trying to fake the family ghost for a critical audience. She said, in her forthright way, 'What's up? Don't you think it's possible?'

I shook my head slowly, in a bemused way, wondering how I could tactfully tip her off without letting Simon know.

She said, 'It has been done before, you know.'

'The night I saw them? Wasn't that the real thing, ma'am?'

'How do I know? I didn't see it, and it certainly wasn't my show, but you aren't going to tell me you believe in ghosts?'

I distrusted that slight smile of hers. I said, 'If I had to stay down in the library alone again in the small hours in a tiny pool of light, I think I'd be ready to believe anything.'

'Oh, so that's the way it is. But I don't think I'll convince your friend Percy like that.'

'He was impressed when he saw how dusty and cobwebby the original candelabra was, ma'am,' I offered.

'Was he, indeed! That young man's no fool,' she remarked.

'But how will you do it?' I asked her, blankly.

'My method,' she said, with a half smile, 'at least, the one I favour at present, is to light the original with nice new candles, and put it behind the screen. Oh, come now, you weren't taken in by the screen in the music room, were you? It's just painted canvas, a rather open mesh, stretched across an alcove. Lit from behind, it will be quite effective.'

I nodded. 'I know I'm being pretty dense, ma'am, but what happens when the press find out it isn't a real ghost, and you've had the money?'

'Oh, you disappoint me,' she said. 'Will they find out? Shall I have had any hand in it? Won't I be as astonished and upset as everyone else? Besides, will there be any proof?'

'Candle-grease?' I suggested. 'Risk of fire? Nosey people snooping in that quarter? Sceptics intent on finding a way to do it without the supernatural creeping in?'

She looked at me for a long minute. 'Very poor-spirited of you,' she said at last. 'Especially when you don't appear to have any better idea.' And before I could comment on that, she murmured, 'By the way, care to tell me just what you did really see, that night?'

I went over it all again for her benefit, but the odd thing was, the more I thought about it, the less I could decide whether I had been chosen to watch a supernatural happening or a beautifully planned hoax. 'It would have had to be Mr Simon, wouldn't it?' I put tentatively.

'Why?' she asked sharply.

'To prove his point? Oh, but then he couldn't know that the chauffeur was going to have an accident, could he? And it was the accident that made the Candles seem so ... so ghostly.'

I looked up at her and she looked really upset. Far more upset than she had been about the threatening letter. I said, 'What is it, Lady Isadora? What have I said?'

She shook her head. 'Think about it. Think what you've suggested,' and she got up and went out of the room.

Her going in that quiet, yet dramatic, fashion, showed me just what I had suggested. I felt sick. Simon couldn't have been responsible for poor old Logsden's fatal accident, could he?

I sat there shaking, thinking. But no, of course, he couldn't. He had come there when I had screamed. He had been standing there all the time, looking at me. He hadn't moved.

But he could have – well, anyone could have – fixed a trip-wire across the stairs, couldn't they, so that Logsden would fall? But for what purpose? Just to prove an old legend? To give weight and truth to the apparition? But why Simon? Much more likely to be Lady Isadora doing such a thing (if anyone in the family could) because she at least had something to gain by it. She could ensure the big sum of money the newspapers were offering, by 'proving' the ghost to be authentic.

I got up and moved about, trying to shake these doubts from my mind. I went up to Sir Hilton's room. He looked up and said, 'Good heavens, don't tell me you've come to work, child?'

I shook my head. 'No, I – I was opening Lady Isadora's mail but I – I thought of something.' I heard myself stammering and saw his jaw drop.

'Better sit down, child. You're ill. Well, you look decidedly under the weather. What happened?'

'I was thinking about the night I saw the Wishbourne Candles – the night the chauffeur died,' I said, with a little rush. 'I don't think I asked you, sir, but did *you* see anything?'

'Yes, you, child, standing down in the hall screaming your head off,' he said promptly.

'But if I may correct you, sir, you didn't *see* that, you heard it – didn't you? I mean, there wasn't a light on, was there?'

He gave it some hard thought. Finally he grinned. 'You're having me on, child! Of course there was a light – it went on behind you. Saw you standing against it. Who did you have in there with you, eh?'

I shook my head, slowly. 'No, I was alone in there. Honestly, I was. With just the table lamp on. That was how it took me so long to get across the room and find the door, because it was dark everywhere else but on the desk. It was so scary, I wouldn't like to do it again.'

He stopped, grinning. 'Must have put the light on yourself, then,' he offered but I said at once, 'How could I? It isn't by the door in the library, is it? I don't think I've discovered where the switch is. Miss Kidby always puts it on. I meant to ask about that.'

'Two-way switch,' he said, after some more thought. 'Someone must have come in by the other door, from the small sitting room.

112

Odd, that, though, because only Lady Isadora uses that room. And she was up on the gallery, right beside me. Oh, I don't know, child, don't worry about it. Stay and take some notes,' he coaxed.

'I can't. I'd love to, but I can't. You see, depending on that light, depends on whether the Candles were a hoax.'

He snorted with delight. 'Well, of course they're a hoax! Good heavens, don't expect me to sit here so easily if they weren't, do you? Wouldn't stay in this damned draughty place another minute if they weren't!'

I gasped. 'You know it's a hoax, for sure, and you're going to let the newspapers pay for the story?'

'Ah, well, no, get your facts right, my dear. Not my doing, so you can't say I'm letting the press pay us – nothing to do with me. Lady Isadora, and she thinks it's the real thing.'

'But, sir, that doesn't make it right, or honest!'

He leaned across the desk and patted my hand. 'You're a nice little thing,' he said, smiling, 'but m'dear, we're not nice or honest, we're the last lot of a very old family and we're as hard up as can be and we're fighting tooth and nail to keep this old pile going, because it's ours, our roots are here, we don't want to have to sell it and go and live in some damned gimmicky cottage or take a flat in Town. Hate that. So would the others,' he said gloomily. 'Still, don't think too badly of us. I never cheated in my life, though I might look the other way if one of the family did. As to the Candles, well, I expect someone's having a bit of a lark and if the press pays us for a story (which I doubt if they'll believe!) who's to refuse it?'

'But it wouldn't be right, would it? And if you were found out, wouldn't that be a lot worse?'

He laughed. 'Lord, no. Lots of people cut up larks to get publicity (which leads to cash) or sell out a story, to the best of their knowledge. That's the way it is, so I'm told. I don't know, mind. Never done it myself. Pinning my faith to this little lot catching on and proving a bestseller. Of course, there are some people – the rest of my family, for example – who will tell you I'm a bit weak in the upper story for having such notions, but there, haven't we all? I bet you aim to marry some chap with expectations of money, now, don't you? Confess it! So what's the difference?'

'I have no such expectations, Sir Hilton,' I

said, in a stony voice. 'How could I? I don't even know who I am. But I know I wouldn't cheat to get big money out of the press and I'm quite sure I wouldn't joke about a ghost, because of frightening people.'

His smile vanished again. He got up and came and stood close to me, looking very seriously down at me. 'No, I know you wouldn't,' he said, and smoothed back his grizzelled hair with an exasperated gesture. 'As I said, you're a nice little thing. I hope you won't be frightened or hurt, while you're under this roof.' He thought some more about it and said suddenly, 'Wouldn't think of going, I suppose? Well, no-one would be surprised. The other typists all cleared out. You could, too. It would be sensible, you know.'

'Why would it? Nobody's going to hurt me, Sir Hilton. Besides, I like being here. I like you all. I want to help, if I can.'

He snorted with laughter. 'How can you help to clear two thou – which is what I owe? Lord knows how much Rex owes. Won't let on. Poor old Isadora is in deep water, too, though she pretends she isn't. As for Simon–'

'Oh, he isn't in debt,' I said quickly, yet heaven knew I had no knowledge to enable me to say any such thing.

115

Sir Hilton wandered off to stare out of the window. 'Simon, now,' he said slowly, 'is a different proposition. Never been the same since that accident. Not reliable, you know. Poor chap, used to like him.'

'Used to?' I took him up.

'Yes, well, how you can get on with a chap who looks at you as if he's never seen you before, when you've been speaking to him half an hour since, beats me. Wilful as ever, though, and tricky tempered. Ever thought, m'dear, that that newspaper man was a nice chap? Your style, I'd think. Percy What His Name – oh, ah, Drewett.'

'What you're doing, Sir Hilton, is to fear I shall have designs on your nephew Simon, and you want me to get interested in someone else. That's it, isn't it? Don't worry, I shan't fall in love with him.'

It was all very fine, saying that, because it was just like turning on a sprinkler valve. I could feel the tears tipping over my lids and pouring down my cheeks, and my lips wobbling, and I just stood there, biting hard on them and wondering how long it would be before I had to take to my heels and rush out of the room.

He came over to me again, and put up one hand, wiping the tears from my cheeks with a soft slow movement of his finger tips. 'No use, m'dear. I know you're in love with him. Young women, thank heaven, aren't much different nowadays than when I was young. They still have a lamp lit behind the eyes, when they're in love, and that's what you have, you know. Makes you look dashed pretty. But you're wrong – over Simon, I mean. You'll get hurt. He's … just not the same chap as he used to be.'

It might have got interesting, only the door opened. Lady Isadora stood there. She said, in her booming voice, 'No need to do that, Hilton – the girl keeps a clean handkerchief on her person. Seen it myself! Come on, Carey, let's work, girl. You'll feel better.'

She marched off. Sir Hilton pulled a funny face, patted my shoulder and pushed me towards the door. He really was an old dear, I reflected, as I rushed after Lady Isadora.

She didn't say anything about it, I found, to my great relief. What she did say, with sly satisfaction, was, 'Just seen that reporter – Percy Thingummy – says we'll get our money if he sees the ghostly Candles just once. Well, he shall, but keep it under your hat.'

Oh, how this family scared me! She gave

me no chance to question her. She just rattled away at her letters and lecture notes, and in working hard, as she had predicted, I forgot my recent tears and almost forgot Simon.

But nothing would let me forget him for long, least of all himself. Half way through the morning, Percy knocked on the door. Lady Isadora boomed 'Come in!' and went right on dictating, until he said, in his deceptively placid voice, 'Sorry to interrupt, ma'am, but the photographer's here – our chap, you know – got a lift from the station off your nephew Simon.'

Chapter Eight

Poor Percy had no idea how much consternation attended that remark of his. It threw Lady Isadora into a terrible state. She didn't make a hysterical noise, of course. She just seemed to wilt, silently, her majestic figure seeming to shrink. I was rather scared.

'Are you all right, ma'am?' I asked her. 'Had I better get you something? Some brandy?'

The mere suggestion pulled her together. 'Don't be a fool, girl! I'm not going to collapse. I shouldn't wonder if I did, though, with such a thing being thrown at me! What is Simon thinking about, tempting Fate like that?'

Percy was apologetic but bland. 'All our chap's fault, ma'am, I'm afraid,' he explained gracefully. 'He heard someone say it was the Wishbourne car so he rather thrust himself upon the driver, instead of waiting for a cab. Might have been a long wait,' he said on consideration.

'You know very well what the significance

of giving a lift in this family, should mean,' Lady Isadora said tartly, 'or you should do, the time you've hung about in this house and probed for information,' so that set Percy down nicely. He pulled a face at me and invited me to come and superintend the putting up of the cameras, so that Lady Isadora shouldn't be disturbed. She said it might be as well if we both took ourselves off and gave her a bit of peace in which to think.

I said wrathfully to Percy, when we were well away from her hearing, that he should be ashamed of himself. 'She isn't all that young, you know. You'll give her a heart attack!'

'Don't talk rot, Carey,' he begged me. 'She's a tough old bird. But I didn't fetch you out of there to discuss your boss, or to help me with something my own chaps can do quite well. I wanted to tell you we want you in the show.'

That shook me. *'Me?'* I gasped. 'Why me?'

'It's very simple,' he said. 'Quite logical, whichever way you look at it. You were the only one to see the Candles. You know where.'

'But that isn't to say I shall see them again,' I said feebly.

'No,' he allowed. 'But it follows. Besides, that's what the big boss on my paper wants. It's news value, anyway. Pretty young girl, in respectable job, caught up in all this wickedness.'

'Wickedness?' I whispered, appalled. Did he *know?*

'Yes, well,' he said comfortably, with one of his nice smiles, 'when you sit round your own cosy fireside one morning, knocking back corn flakes and egg and bacon and it's snowing or foggy outside, you feel better for reading about ghosts and things in a castle on the cliffs if the victim is a girl like yourself. See what I mean?'

'Yes,' I said, weakly, thinking briefly of such a picture as he had painted, in my own life before Tom Brewster had captivated the person I had called 'mother' for all my life, and ruined everything for us both. I said, 'I wish none of it was going to happen. I wish I hadn't come here.'

'Well, it's an ill wind,' Percy said sensibly. 'If you hadn't, I doubt if I'd have had this chance of advancement in my job, and I mightn't have met you, and I'd have been the poorer for that.' He gave me such a nice smile. I remembered it afterwards, but I didn't pay much attention then. He didn't give me a chance. He hustled me up the back stairs, talking all the time. 'I've found something up here and I want to show you and this time we won't have interruptions like the time before when your dear Simon jumped on us, because I've discovered his little way in, and I've blocked it up.'

'You haven't.' I stood still with shock but Percy wasn't having that. 'Come on,' he said, 'Don't waste time or someone will discover that their tame stenographer isn't tapping a typewriter and then you'll have to leave me and I shall hate that before I've shown you what I found.'

'How is it you were allowed to search and find anything without someone discovering?' I asked him.

'Ah, well, you see,' he said, as we reached the top of the spiral staircase and he shut the attic door behind us and bolted it. 'It's one of my natural gifts – so my boss says. You see, I've got a trick of leaning against the wall and looking restful and someone comes along and needs a bit of help and says to me, "Hold this chum" and I'm willing, and I find myself in the middle of someone else's job or problem and I've got a story. Simple as that. Of course, if you go about looking like everyone thinks a reporter should look, there are times when people fade away or just shut up like a clam.'

'Who says "Hold this, chum" in this place?' I asked suspiciously.

'Well, I don't know who he is exactly and I didn't ask because through him taking advantage of my good nature, I indirectly found what I'm going to show you,' and he went confidently to a child's gaudy painted toy cupboard and opened it. There, inside it, was a branched candelabra, the exact copy of the one suspended from the ceiling. That one was covered in cobwebs and dust, but this was clean, shiny ... no, *shining,* I amended to myself, as I stood in front of it blocking the daylight and it still glowed as if a light was on it. I put out a finger to touch it but Percy stopped me.

'I wouldn't, if I were you, unless you want your fingertip to glow in the dark. Phosphorus paint, and not long been done.'

He closed the toy cupboard and stood up. I said blankly, 'Do you mean to tell me you were invited to help a man paint that thing? Just like that?'

'No, not exactly. He came and got it, took it away, brought it back again. I was required to help him move that wardrobe,' and he indicated a huge old-fashioned piece of furniture weighing half a ton, I should think, 'from in front of the toy cupboard. I had taken off my jacket,' Percy said modestly, 'and my sleeves were rolled up and I expect I looked rather dirty, or else this chap wouldn't have mistaken me for one of the other servants. I would think he came from outside.'

'What did he look like?' I asked, and in horror I listened to Percy describing the old fisherman who lived in the cottage where Simon's horse was usually tethered.

'Surprised?' Percy asked gently.

I nodded. Percy said, 'Now Carey, let's have it. You aren't really. You expected something of the sort, didn't you?'

'Oh, why did you have to come here?' I burst out. 'No, I didn't expect … well, yes, I did, but it isn't like you think!'

I held my hands to my head. I had to say something but I couldn't give the family away – they had my loyalty and I didn't understand why. It wasn't all because of Simon. But at the same time I didn't feel it was right for this young man – and his newspaper – to be cheated. I struggled briefly with myself, then said, 'The thing is, I believe the family is pretty scared that there might be some truth in the legend, so they're going to cook up their own version just to – well, tell themselves they don't believe in ghosts, sort of thing.'

It sounded feeble and Percy shook his head. 'You'll have to do better than that, Carey.'

'I can't,' I said miserably. 'It's to do with Simon. He's a bit peculiar since a piece of rock fell from the Cave of Gold and hit him on the head.'

'A piece of what?' Percy said incredulously. 'What nonsense is this?' so I told him what I knew of Simon's accident.

'Well, I think I can explode that one, by showing you the big thing I'd kept up my sleeve!'

He shut the child's toy cupboard, and I noticed he left everything else just as it had been. He caught my close look and he laughed. 'Miss Kidby keeps everything written in her little book. She'd know if anything had been moved.'

'You mean she's in it, too? The new candelabra, I mean?'

'Oh, no,' Percy said quickly. 'But the toy cupboard is just as she left it so she won't expect any such thing to be in it. She doesn't, you know. She's never heard of people being able to pick a simple lock.' He caught my glance. 'I had it unlocked ready for you.'

He took me to the end of the attics, near where the wide stairs were. Here the heavy furniture was transported. We went down these and into the passage below. No-one was about. All the housework for the day had been completed – Miss Kidby kept the maids up to time like a good sergeant major. In the silence of that dark corridor I was astonished to see Percy slip round the corner of the stairs, do something at the panelled wall, where a hole appeared, and slip through. The hole was made by one panel going inwards, like a small low door. He put out a hand and yanked me through, shutting it behind him.

'But–' I began, in astonishment.

He laughed. 'You don't read any of the books in the library here, do you?'

'You found out about this in a book?' I gasped.

He nodded. 'It's nothing. Apparently in the old smuggling days Wishbourne was in the brandy racket with the rest of the village. Don't you remember the old song, about the parson and the clerk taking their share?'

I was horrified. 'But the family can't know about this!'

Percy was sceptical. 'I bet they do. Just take it for granted, I expect. Probably forgotten about it.'

'But – where does it lead to?'

He shrugged. 'Your Cave of Gold you're always on about.'

As we went down dusty stone steps that muffled all sound, I thought about it, and refuted such an idea. 'No, I've been there. There's no possible exit other than that on the shore.'

'Yes, I know, like there's no need to doubt a rock falling on someone's head in the main chamber. When we get there, just take a look at the cave's ceiling.'

'*If* we get there,' I said. 'Anyway, aren't you afraid Simon or the old fisherman will be coming up and catch us?'

'I looked out of the attic window just before we came down,' Percy said. 'They're both at the cottage. The horse is tethered there.'

He thought of everything. But he was so wrong about this, I comforted myself.

But he wasn't. We came out eventually between two rocks in the passage leading to the main chamber. I wondered how I could have missed it, except that no-one looks for anything much in a dark passage when there is an interesting big room at the end.

Percy had brought a torch and he flashed it round. There was no evidence of food or anything today. Percy nudged me and jerked the torch upwards. 'A rock fell on him from the ceiling, I think you said?'

I looked up, and got a shock. The whole ceiling was perfectly smooth. Not by natural means but by bricking up, using the local stone. 'Shored up, ages ago,' he murmured, 'but too smooth and firm at the moment to admit of an accident. I would favour that,' and he showed in his torch beam a ledge I hadn't noticed. It was used to keep oddments of supplies but I thought I saw what Percy was getting at. The ledge was wide enough for someone to crouch and throw something down. 'Someone didn't like your Simon, I would say,' Percy hazarded, before he led the way out.

'But I don't see where it gets us,' I protested, as we toiled up the steps to the passage and the attics.

'Neither do I, at the moment,' Percy admitted, 'except that it's quite clear your Simon uses that way in and out, and it seems odd, doesn't it, when there's a good front door?'

'He *is* odd since the accident. I told you,' I

said crossly.

We didn't have any more time to discuss such things. Lady Isadora sent for me. She had a lot more rubbish to be burnt in the cellars and Mr Rex had left a lot of taped stuff for me to type. Simon came in, in a foul temper, and the press people had set their cameras up and Miss Kidby said they were in the way and why couldn't they wait until nightfall.

I wasn't really looking forward to the next performance of the Candles. I really felt I should warn the family, in case they all tried to put on a separate show. But on thinking it over, it appeared there was only one duplicate set and that was in the toy cupboard, so presumably they had left everything to Simon this time.

None the less, I felt impelled to say something when he came down into the cellars later and commiserated with me on the dirty job I had again been given.

He stood in the doorway just as he had on the other occasion, his brown eyes hidden behind the dark glasses. He took them off and said abruptly, 'Carey how is it you get all the dirty jobs? Why can't the maids do that?'

So, I thought, with a little flutter of

pleasure, he's in his nice mood again, and I prepared to enjoy it.

'It's private and personal stuff. I don't mind doing this,' I said. 'Don't worry. What I am concerned about is the haunting.'

'Oh, that!' he dismissed it as of nothing. 'As boys, we used to go down late at night and sit on the stairs and wait but we never saw a thing.'

'We? Who is the we?' I asked. I desperately wanted to know.

His face closed. 'This was a big family in those days. There were other young people my age,' but it had the chilling quality of telling me to shut up.

'I'm sorry,' I said.

'What for?'

'For saying something to make you go away from me.'

After a startled moment, he came over, slowly, and stood just behind me. Close, so close, that I could feel his warm breath on my neck, and I began to tingle all over, only the tingling was pleasant. I wanted him to kiss me because on this occasion I was sure I should like it.

As I waited, holding my breath, he said on a low note, 'Little Carey Constable, for heaven's sake tell me what happened between us to make you say such a thing.'

I put the poker down and turned to him. 'Don't you remember you kissed me? Was it so casual – just like kissing the housemaid, or have you just … forgotten?'

I hadn't meant such anguish to creep into my voice, but it did. I heard it. He seemed to blindly put his arms round me but he didn't kiss me then. He just held me close to him and put his cheek on the top of my head, and I heard him say (or I thought I heard him say) 'I hope to heaven I haven't down anything to … hurt you.'

The situation was getting out of hand, only in a different way this time. I said, with a forced cheerfulness, 'Don't be silly, of course you didn't. You wouldn't! It's just that you did kiss me and then the next time you see me, you snub me, and … I can't take it.'

I didn't mean to make it so apparent how I felt. I don't think I realized myself how much I had come to cherish those moments spent with him. Heaven knew there hadn't been so many, but it was like having a rock to lean on, someone to care a little about me. Yet it troubled me that there were times when I didn't even like him. I didn't try to separate those times from this time, however; he would soon take it into his head to go. So I said, 'Don't mind me. It's my first resident job and among strangers and ... well, *you* know!'

'I know,' he agreed, then he turned my face up with one finger. 'I'm no good to you, Carey. What good is a man who can't even remember when he kisses a girl? But for what it's worth, I'll kiss you now,' and he did.

You would think a kiss was just a kiss but it isn't, I discovered then. That was a starting kiss, a kiss that has a first time, and his mouth didn't bruise mine as it had on those other occasions. He looked at me to see how I had taken it, and somehow we went on fire and he seemed surprised at himself. He kissed me in a way that blotted out the kissing in the cave, and we were both shaking when I came up for air.

He smoothed my hair back and said thickly, 'Whatever I may say on other occasions, don't mind. This is as it really is. I meant it. Remember that, won't you?' and he let me go and walked out.

He almost went straight into the wall but remembered in time and put out a hand to steady himself but what with the memory of that last time when he had crashed into the wall, and the effect of his kisses this time, I forgot to warn him about what was happening regarding the Candles.

Chapter Nine

I was cross about that, and cross that I hadn't spoken to him about the secret way down to the cave although, all things considered, perhaps it was as well.

But most of all I was astonished and put out because of the change in him and the way his kisses had affected me. If only he could be like that all the time! That wretched accident of his had spoilt his life and mine too. The next time I saw him, he not only snapped my head off but gave me a look of such withering contempt that I couldn't believe he had been so sweet that second time in the cellars.

Not that I had much time for thinking. When the press takes over, there is no time or opportunity for anything.

I don't know when I first became aware that Percy liked me a little too much. I suppose it was Lady Isadora who pointed it out to me.

She had called me to her room when she was dressing for dinner that night. 'Help me on with these, child,' she said, 'while I talk to you. Tonight's the night, and I feel somehow that the full regalia must be on, to meet our ghost.'

'You're laughing about it, ma'am, and I wish you wouldn't,' I said earnestly. 'No, don't look at me like that. I'm not the sort of person to believe in ghosts, and I can't honestly say I felt any evil down there in the darkness that night when I saw it, but there was something, or *someone*. It couldn't appear by itself, I'm sure, so that means that someone made it appear, and if it wasn't you or Sir Hilton or Mr Rex or Mr Simon, then *who?*'

She looked at me with real interest then. She looked very nice. No, perhaps *nice* wasn't the word. She looked splendid. I don't see how it was achieved because she could hardly be called a good-looking woman, but it was her manner, I suppose. I had never seen her out of tweeds, mannish suits and starkly tailored dresses before. Tonight she wore a velvet gown of – plum? No, a reddish purple, and her maid had set her hair. She wore the Wishbourne dia-monds, a set I knew were kept under lock and key unless it was a very special occasion indeed. The long earrings made her look even taller, more regal, and although she wasn't going so far as to wear the tiara, she had the diamond collar and the bracelet, and I couldn't keep the admiration out of my eyes.

She dashed me by saying, 'They're only paste, child. We had to sell the diamonds long ago,' and the tone in her voice made a catch come in my throat.

'Mr Simon says he honestly believes there is gold in the cave. I hope you find it,' I said, idly. It was the best I could do to offer comfort, though I didn't really believe it myself.

It had a curious effect on her, at any rate. Her head shot up and she met my eyes in the glass. 'What did you say?' she asked.

'He honestly believes it's there, although he looked sorry he said the cave, and altered it to somewhere else. I think he means the cave, though.'

'No, not Simon, never *Simon*,' she whispered, her cheeks ashen.

'What have I said, ma'am?' I gasped. She looked ill.

With her head shaking, she said twice over, 'Not Simon. Not Simon. He's the one who is always saying it isn't anywhere. It's a pipe dream.'

'Well, I know in some moods he says that,

but at other times he says very firmly that it's there and he's going to find it,' I said, a little less certainly.

She still looked ill. It almost threw her off balance and made her forget what she had sent for me for.

'Look, child, this Percy What's His Name – he likes you. You know that as well as I do,' she began, not meeting my eyes.

'He likes everyone,' I said and I believed that. He was the most cheerful amiable sort of young man I had ever met.

'You specially. I've seen the way he looks at you,' she insisted. ' And I did wonder, bearing in mind how much tonight means to us – well, to me, anyway – I wondered– Good heavens, what's the matter with me? Why can't I ask you outright?'

'Ask me what, ma'am? I'll do anything for you, within reason.'

'Thanks for the "within reason",' she said shortly. 'Perhaps you won't think it is! Well, the point is, we're rigging it. You know it. You must also know that if it is photographed, what will happen to us. Very well, then, I want something to happen, a diversion to be caused, at that point. Think you could faint or something?'

I looked at her with my mouth open, I

think. She continued, impatiently, 'Well, you know yourself, my dear, that if you collapsed, he'd look at you and not at the Candles.'

'But he won't be taking the picture,' I pointed out.

'Then collapse against his photographer,' she retorted. 'Will you do that for me? Well, then, for Simon! He stands to gain just as much for this night's work, in a rather different way.'

'How?' I asked coldly.

She sighed. 'Oh, dear, this is going to be so difficult. I knew from the start that you'd have a conscience. Well, let's get it over. If you've got a ghost, or the suggestion of one, you can benefit financially in several ways. Now do stop looking indignant, my dear. You are not from a very old family and you've no idea what it's like to have a small historical mansion to keep up. It isn't big enough or important enough to bequeath it to a grateful nation, but it's too big for our slender purses. And if you don't think I loathe having to let you know all this, you're not the intelligent girl I think you are!'

'I do know all that and I begin to see what it means,' I could say with great sincerity, because I was in love with Simon, and his outlook was my own interest. But she wasn't to know that.

'Yes, well, very nice. The thing is, there's a ghost-laying society from a small town in America, over here at the moment. You may not know the ffanchard-Yeedons, but they've had this little lot at Yeedon Holt for a blissful three weeks and they're considerably better off for it. Following on that, a woman's magazine is getting interested, and a top flight novelist thinks he would like to stay there one or two nights and use their ghost in his new novel.

'*Have* they got a ghost, ma'am?' I asked bluntly.

'That isn't the point, my dear. Oh, well, if you must press for an answer, there is a sort of blur that keeps coming out in photographs, whatever that may prove. The thing is, everyone is satisfied and shows their satisfaction with a flattering financial generosity, which is what we want. I fancy that the story of the Candles will do a lot for us.'

'I think it's awful,' I said hotly, 'commercialising it!'

'Everyone does, if they have anything to commercialise,' she said.

Nothing could shift her, but then nothing could shift me. I would not promise to do anything to spoil Percy's picture or his story, although he was only doing it for the money, too.

I felt that if only I could find Simon and talk with him, it would help. But I couldn't find him anywhere and I had so much work to do that I dare not waste too much time.

I had my evening meal with the housekeeper and she told me about other houses she had worked in. 'Not that I believe in ghosts,' she said carefully, 'but there was one at a Tudor house called Meckham Grange, and I left next morning. To my shame I say it, I wouldn't stay there another night. Not that there was much to see, mind you, but it was the *feeling*. Everything went icy cold, and I don't mind telling you, my dear, when I saw this bit of mist in the distance and someone said it was the ghost, I was never so frightened in my life! My legs wouldn't work. I wanted to run but I couldn't.'

'What happened?' I asked, my mind on the second candelabra.

'I fainted, and someone else carried me away. I was only nineteen and I never have fancied being about in the small hours since. But I must say that the night I heard you screaming, it didn't *feel* the same.' She looked earnestly at me. 'Not like Meckham Grange at all. No *evil*.'

She was a good soul but I was glad to get away from her garrulity. I accidentally bashed right into Percy as I rounded a corner of the top landing. He caught my hands and held them. 'Where are *you* going to be tonight, Carey?' he asked me.

'Why? I've got my instructions. I can't alter them.'

'I hope you're to stay in your room,' he said rather grimly.

'Well, I'm not. I've been told just where I'm to be, in the thick of it.'

'Where?' Percy asked gently, but I had discovered in the past that his gentle questions usually made people answer at the double. I did then. 'I have to stand by the cameras,' I said.

'Then I shall stand by you, love. And where will Master Simon be?'

'You don't like him, do you?' I marvelled.

'Neither do you, all the time,' he said shrewdly.

I was near tears again. It was hateful to think that I wore my heart on my sleeve like that. Supposing Sir Hilton and Mr Rex had noticed? I fancied Sir Hilton had, anyway.

Percy put his arm round my shoulder in a brotherly way. 'I wish you wouldn't get upset when someone puts a facer to you,' he said kindly. 'I know what it's like to be so fond of someone and to realise they don't care a button.'

I looked up at him in amazement, my face all wet. 'You do?' I gasped.

'Yes, I do,' he told me, looking at me so kindly that my tears flowed again. I was fed-up with myself but I couldn't stop. The fact that Simon could be so nice, and yet so hateful, and never seem to realise it, was tearing me apart.

Percy pulled me gently to him and let me weep on his waistcoat, while he stroked the back of my hair and said a few things. I don't know what he was saying, but I felt awful that I was commissioned to cheat him when the Candles appeared.

I felt a lot better for his kindness and was just going to straighten up when I heard someone walk by. Percy, who never let anyone bother him about ceremony or respect or things like that, didn't move, but I was considerably put out when I saw the stiff back of Simon. What must he have thought of me? 'Oh,' I exploded to Percy, 'why didn't you *say* he was coming along?'

Percy said very sensibly, 'I don't suppose it will make much difference, love, because he won't do any of the things you might want him to. His aunt said he's fixed to marry some wealthy girl whose father owns a couple of shipping lines. That's if he can bring her to accept him, that is.'

'I don't believe it,' I fumed. But of course, it was likely, and anyway, as I had already told myself, what was there in it for me, with *anyone?*

I didn't really expect Simon to take any notice of me that evening after that. I wandered through the hall where Mike Edritch was fiddling with his beloved camera, and Percy was prowling. Percy went up the grand staircase and leaned over, then came down and looked up. He put something on the table, then moved it a foot. All the time he talked to Mike and they both ignored me.

I said, 'What makes you think the Candles will appear on the table?' and I wondered if I had given away too much. Lady Isadora had mentioned the tightly drawn painted canvas panels each side of the fireplace, which were supposed to house a place for the candelabra to be. Percy said, 'I'm hoping.'

'Because that was where I said I'd seen them,' I said.

'No, because that was where you said you

saw them,' he corrected.

I found Sir Hilton calmly sorting through some notes for the next day's work. He looked up. 'My dear!' he said, and I knew my eyes were still red.

'I've been bawling again,' I said briefly. 'I came to see if there was something I could do, in this room. I don't want to be alone. Do you mind, sir?'

'Delighted, m'dear. Glad you don't run off to m'brother Rex every time!' The idea was so ludicrous that it made me laugh and Sir Hilton laughed, too. He put his notes away.

'Oh, what do we want to work tonight for? We're all on edge. Talk, now. Tell me about your family.'

'But I told you – I haven't got a family. I'm a foundling,' I said.

'Sorry, m'dear, I forgot. But haven't you tried to find out who– Well, no, perhaps you haven't. But won't it be awkward when you marry? A man likes to know who– Well, perhaps I'm being supremely tactless.'

I looked out of the window. I didn't know why I had come here to him, except that I sensed that no-one wanted me, until the show started. I said as much.

Sir Hilton examined his silver pencil. 'As a matter of fact, I've thought better of it. I'm doing nothing this night.'

'Might I ask why, sir?'

'Oh, I don't know. I feel restless, not in tune for such things. We've had one death. I'm a bit depressed tonight. Can't think why.'

'Sir Hilton, have you got a book in here with a plan of the house?'

'Funny you should say that! There used to be such a book in the library. I was looking for it, but it's gone.'

'Probably that reporter still has it. He's been reading it.'

'Has he though!'

'Yes, have you ever read it, Sir Hilton?' I urged.

'No. I never bothered. I don't believe any of us did, after one of the boys tried to find a secret passage and fell through into the stables and broke his leg. It was all bricked up so don't go looking for it.'

'Oh,' I said. 'What boys? Do you mind me asking? Families (now I don't belong to one) have a morbid curiosity for me.'

He seemed ready enough to talk. 'We were a happy family in those days,' he said. 'There was me, and my brother Rex, of course, and Lady Isadora. Our mother was a Holford, you understand.' He leaned back and smiled at me, because I suppose I was showing undue interest. 'Her two brothers lived here then, with their boys.'

'Two boys?' I asked with baited breath.

He shook his head. 'Four boys. It was a cheerful noisy place in those days in the school holidays, of course. A nice place for young boys to live in.'

'Four boys! So that's what Simon meant by "we",' I murmured half to myself.

He looked sharply at me, but said nothing about that. 'My mother was also Isadora. Confusing, no doubt,' he continued after a while. 'One of her brothers was Rex. Paucity of choice of names in this family. Of the four boys, one was Hilton, one Rex, two Simons.'

'Two Simons!' I sat up with a jerk.

'Yes,' he said, sourly. 'Good thing they didn't look alike. It would have been tiresome. Well, of course, one was Simon Nicholas, went by the nick-name of Nick. Red, like his mother. Red as fire. Red as his mother, and she was a beauty.' He went off in a dream no doubt thinking of the beautiful redhead who had been the mother of Simon Nicholas. I hated to wrench him back, but I had to.

'Where is he now, the other Simon, I mean?'

'What? Oh, gone! Unfortunate family, this. All of 'em gone. The war claimed some (air-raids took some of the women off) and a plane accident did for young Hilton. Then young Rex got killed in a shooting accident at school. Bad show, that. No, all we have left is me and m'brother, and young Simon, more's the pity.'

'What do you mean?' I breathed.

'Well, look at him. Not right in the head, whatever way you choose to look at it,' he said fiercely to me.

He knows for sure that I'm silly about him, I thought, and I was glad to go. I got up and left him, wishing I hadn't gone to speak to him. Much better to see him bluff and hearty, dictating his work with an intensity and enthusiasm that blotted everything else out, rather than to let him age with the sadness of his memories, such as now, remembering the other young people, and the beautiful woman whom someone else had married, but both of them had loved.

Anyway, when I went downstairs, I was required to busy myself, and somehow the hours until twelve thirty slipped by. I know I had begun to yawn, to wonder if I could slip up the back stairs and go to bed, when the bell buzzed. It was a signal for me to go out into the hall. Percy was to tread on the buzzer, and he trod on it so viciously that I almost screamed out with shock.

I stumbled to the door, as I had on that other occasion, but this time, believing that Lady Isadora had rigged the thing, I was more critically interested than afraid. And there it was, just as before, an eerie thing, glowing, rather too blurred to be beautiful. I was shocked into immobility. I knew at the back of my mind that I was supposed to get near Mike Edritch and faint all over him and his camera but I couldn't move. I just had to watch the thing and see how it would vanish.

It was Lady Isadora who provided the commotion needed to take our attention off the thing. She shouted: 'Simon! Oh, *no!*' and fell to the floor. She was a big woman and whatever she did was not quiet. We all looked, and when we looked back, of course, the thing had gone.

'Lights!' someone yelled. (I think it was Percy). But of course, the main switch had been fused. The thing had been well done. Percy struggled with something in his pocket and brought out a torch, but of course, by then, there was nothing to be seen, and then all the lights came on. Percy swooped to the table, disregarding the group of servants and family round Lady Isadora, trying to revive her. Percy wanted to see what I was anxious about – candle-grease on the table. But there wasn't any. There wasn't anything to indicate that something had been there, and I must say he looked a bit queasy for a moment. I know I felt it, even though I knew it had been rigged – or they had *said* they were going to rig it. Now my own doubts crept in. Was it possible to rig the thing so slickly?

It was then that I remembered Lady Isadora, and I found, with some dismay, that she had really passed out. It wasn't faked. No-one could look so ashen and so ill as she did just then. I forgot about Percy and the Candles, in helping the maids get her to her room. The last I heard of it was Percy shouting to his cameraman to get those pictures developed at the double. But as we helped her on to her bed, Lady Isadora said something rather odd. 'Simon is out of his mind. I must think again.'

Chapter Ten

Past experience with elderly relatives of the person I knew as Mother, led me to the conviction that nothing would make Lady Isadora repeat that remark. Whether the collapse was real or feigned, these older ladies all seemed to have a sixth sense about repeating things which were blurted out in the heat of the moment. We got her on to her bed and made her drink some brandy, suggested extra blankets, hot bottles, the visit of the doctor, the sending for Sir Hilton or Mr Rex, or even Simon, and all these things were condemned by the invalid with a degree of ferocity which put us all at ease as to the speed of her recovery. Colour was coming back into her cheeks. I felt I could reasonably send the maids away. But I stayed.

Lady Isadora lay quietly with her eyes closed for a while, then she cautiously opened them to see who was still in the room. 'Oh, it's you, Carey Constable! What are you being so faithful for?'

I grinned weakly at her. 'Don't know,

ma'am,' I allowed. 'Just worried about you.'

'Yes, I believe that to be true, but why? That's what I want to know. Nobody ever worried about me before.'

'You didn't throw a faint,' I said softly, and watched to see how she took that. 'It was real.'

'What makes you think so?' she countered fiercely.

I looked at my hand. The fingers were still on her pulse, which hadn't quietened down as much as I would have liked. 'Take your hand away,' she said angrily. 'You're not a nurse, are you?'

'No, but I was a Girl Guide,' I told her firmly. 'I know enough about First Aid to know that you had a very bad shock.'

'So it's no use my denying it,' she observed. 'But you won't be fool enough to expect me to tell you what it was, I trust?'

'I'd like to,' I admitted. 'But I won't. It was something to do with Simon, though. You sounded so ... agonized, when you called out to him. I didn't even see him.'

'Didn't you?' she observed sourly, then added, 'I wish you had. I could have checked with you.'

'I was looking at the Candles,' I told her. 'I had promised myself I would watch them to see how they vanished, but you fainted and took my attention away.'

'Let's hope I managed to take other people's attention away too,' she observed devoutly. 'I thought I asked *you* to fall on the camera?'

'I'm sorry,' I apologized, 'but I forgot. I don't think I would have, even if I hadn't forgotten.'

'Oh, lor, that's all we need,' she said, closing her eyes. 'You've fallen in love with Percy What's His Name.'

'No, I haven't,' I told her. And if she was going to be dramatic, there was no reason why I shouldn't, either. Anyway, Sir Hilton would probably betray me to her, so I said, 'If you want to know, it's Simon. You can send me away if you like, but I can't help it.'

I didn't manage to achieve a cold and dignified pronouncement though. It made me furious, but there it was: my wretched voice went thick and broke off.

She glanced quickly at me. 'Oh, no!' she moaned. 'That's beyond everything. Why, child, why?' And before I could answer, she sat up on her elbow, knocking my questing fingers away from her pulse impatiently, and said, 'Well, you must know too, then!'

I didn't realize, even then, what she was

talking about. I said miserably, 'I know I'm not likely to get anything out of it. I ought to go away. Anyway, for my own peace of mind, I ought to go away, because sometimes I love him, and sometimes I think I hate him. I don't understand it. I only know I just can't bear it.'

She looked so distressed. She looked as if she were making up her mind to say something, but at that moment someone knocked and opened the door a crack, and said, 'May I come in, Aunt?'

She said, 'Yes, do, you're the one we want to see,' and Simon came in. My dear Simon. I stood hastily and looked at him. His dark glasses were dangling in his hand. He flinched a little at the light and hastily put them on, but he was looking at me, not his aunt, as he did so.

'Carey, I wish you'd leave us,' he said quietly.

Lady Isadora said quickly, 'No! Not for a moment. There's something I must do. I want to see the scar, Simon.'

He looked rather odd, but he bent down obligingly, and she moved his fair hair, and there it was. Still a rather livid weal. I felt my tummy lurch in sympathy as I realized what a blow it must have been. But she need not have done that. I knew it would be there. I didn't understand much else, but I did know, in case she felt he hadn't told the truth about that accident, that it had been true, and never mind if the cave roof was smooth, somehow a rock had found its way to his head.

'All right, Carey, you can go now,' Lady Isadora said. 'And see if you can find out about those press pictures.'

Simon said, 'That's what I came to tell you, Aunt. They're developed. Satisfactory results, I understand. You'll get your money and more, by the sounds they are making.'

He sounded as if he didn't approve, as well he might. I went out, very much shaken, and encountered Percy getting ready to go. He looked odd: excited, upset – I couldn't tell which.

'Are you going back to London? At this time of night?'

It was his cameraman who answered. 'You bet your sweet life we are, and if you want to know, I'll be glad to see the inside of a pub in Fleet Street after this place!'

I must have looked puzzled. Percy said, 'Show her one of the shots, Mike,' so he did, looking rather glum.

'Well, what are you being so pleased about

that thing for?' I asked blankly. It looked as if someone had grabbed the camera and made it shiver. I said so.

'No,' Mike said. 'Camera steady as a rock. Other things steady in the picture. See the clear outline of the table? Just the old ghost all blurred. I don't know what it means, but it's good enough for me. I need a drink.' He glanced at me. 'Why don't you come back to London with us? You don't want to stop here, do you?' and he glanced at Percy doubtfully.

Percy said, 'Let her do as she likes,' and I don't think he was surprised when I shook my head and said I'd stay.

'Then it's goodbye,' he said, and his cameraman, with unusual tact, took himself out to their terrible old car. I looked at it and said, 'That's funny, you had that all the time, so why did you ask for a lift?' It was really to Mike that I directed the question.

'Percy had the car,' Mike said, and he grinned. From that, I supposed I could deduce that like the family here, the press boys weren't above doing a bit of faking. Probably Percy briefed his cameraman about the legend and meant to use it.

Percy said, 'If you ever need a friend, remember me, Carey? I'll be around. And don't do your "orphan" stunt on me. I don't give a damn what you antecedents are. You're just you.'

I suppose, really, that that was the most modern declaration of love a girl could wish for, and the sweetest. I said thank you in such a husky voice that I wondered if he heard me, but he must have. He bent and briefly kissed me, merely brushing my cheek with his lips, and then, with the comment, 'You know how to contact me if you want me,' he went out into the dark and windy night.

It was the small hours. I wasn't sure of the time really. The night sky had a slightly pearly lustre about it, and the hard glitter of the stars had softened. The wind was noisy rather than harsh, too, and it seemed a pity when the butler came along and quietly shut the door and bolted it and asked if I didn't think I should go to bed.

Bed! What a thought, after all that had happened. But I did, finally, and I overslept, but nobody seemed to mind. The family slept late – that is, all but Simon. I don't know what he did. Probably rose at five thirty as usual and rode that black horse of his. But at ten o'clock we were all brighter than I should have ever thought we could be, because the telephone rang and kept ringing. The story had somehow leaked out.

How do such stories leak out? That was what I wanted to know then, but later I discovered that the newest housemaid had a boy-friend at the local service station, where Percy and his cameraman had had to stop to fill up with petrol. They were known by sight locally and after they had gone, the young man was all agog to know why they were going back to London. All the staff had been sworn to secrecy, but the very tone of the girl's voice as she had assured her young man she was not allowed to say anything, was enough to start speculation. The local newspaper telephoned. The other big houses – their owners all known to be interested in the outcome of Lady Isadora's venture – communicated urgently, and then the Americans came on the line.

I had, of course, no notion of what was going on except from her one-sided conversation but Lady Isadora looked rather sick, I thought. Yet it seemed, from what she said, that the American party were suggesting a generous fee for the opportunity to bring a party of people to stay at Wishbourne Towers, a 'ghosting holiday', they called it. Of course, she was proud. Still, she needed the money badly and I was a little surprised to see her square her shoulders and thrust her chin in the air, as if she were coming to terms with herself, before she agreed on the price suggested and fixed a date and time for them to come.

At last she put the telephone down and said to me, 'They are coming, *nine-strong,* to get a sight of the Wishbourne Candles.'

'Nine other people?' I asked faintly, thinking of Miss Kidby and the shifts she made already to keep all the beds going and to put food on the table of a sort that the family had been used to. 'I see,' I said. There seemed to be nothing else to say! After that, we were in the throes of preparing for that visit, and it created such an upheaval that the account of us in the London papers was something of an anti-climax.

It was Percy's effort really, and I did so much hope that he would get what he deserved, for so much patient work. His cameraman had done a nice job with Wishbourne looking at its absolute worst, on a wet windy day, with the sky reaching down almost to touch the angry sea, and the few starved trees visible beyond the surrounding wall detracting from rather than adding to the general lack of comfort about the place. I could well imagine Percy's readers would decide that the best haunting would be done at Wishbourne, and perhaps for the first time I began to have doubts about the place myself. For after studying Percy's effort, and deciding that the other three old houses weren't really as chilling as ours, I tackled Lady Isadora, and she said categorically that she had had no hand in the performance that night.

I watched her face as she stared at the picture of the Candles. They were so blurred that you could only agree to their being a nine-branched candelabra because it said so. 'If you didn't, ma'am, who did?' I whispered. 'Percy Drewett had a close look for candle-grease afterwards and there wasn't any!'

'There wouldn't be,' she said, and refused to discuss it any more. Neither would Sir Hilton, who had been so friendly on the subject before. As to Mr Rex, he seemed to grow more silent and preoccupied as the days went by. And Simon kept right out of my sight.

It was on the day that the Americans were due to come, that I managed to find him. That was a black day. He was riding back on his horse. Always I had to stop and watch him because horse and rider were so well attuned, they almost seemed to be fused together. His back was straight as a ramrod, yet he didn't bounce up and down. He pulled up and leaned down, lifting his dark glasses, and saying doubtfully, 'Carey?'

I said, 'Yes, can't you really see me, Simon?'

'Not so well today,' he said curtly. 'Do you ride?' and when I said I did, he said, 'Put your foot in this stirrup and come up with me. I'm worried.'

I did so. He pulled me up as easily as if I were a bit of flotsam on the edge of the sea. His great black beast danced a little, protestingly, but he steadied him with a soft word, and we went on at a sedate walk. Simon said, 'I can't find my old friend, Jimmy Noy.'

My heart began to hammer with sickening thuds. Never before had Simon referred to him as his old friend, nor had he ever sounded worried; merely contemptuous.

I said, 'Where you tether the horse?' and he nodded.

So many things rushed into my mind. I said, 'I've wanted to speak to you so much and I couldn't find you,' but he merely said impatiently, 'I've been around. You hadn't time to talk, anyway, the way they rushed you off your legs. Why do you let them?'

My own dear kind Simon, I thought, with a little glow, but it wasn't a big enough glow to chase away the feeling of chill, of wretchedness, that was beginning to clamp down on me.

He was too much preoccupied with the whereabouts of the old fisherman to care about anything else. I said, 'Well, when did you see him last?' and he said, 'Monday.'

Monday. The day the Candles had been rigged, to appear that night. The day Percy had taken me to the attic to show me things.

'Simon,' I said, tentatively, 'the Candles – was it the ghost?'

He didn't answer at first. I said, 'I know the family were going to rig them. Lady Isadora told me why. She didn't want to, but I was supposed to take part, only it wasn't necessary in the end.'

He looked down at me. I wished he would take his glasses off so I could see his eyes, but he didn't.

His silence was unnerving. I said, 'Simon, *did* you?'

'Did I … what?' he asked, very quietly indeed.

'I wouldn't think badly of you if you did something to help alleviate Lady Isadora's anxiety about money, honestly I wouldn't, only tell me – did you take part in it?'

'No, I didn't,' he said slowly. 'I wasn't even there. I was looking for Jimmy.'

'Jimmy took part in it,' I said, in a muffled voice.

'What's that supposed to mean?' he asked, after an odd silence.

'Percy Drewett showed me a second candelabra, hidden in a toy cupboard, and it was painted with phosphorescent paint, and he said Jimmy Noy took it away and brought it back painted. Well, that is to say, he described Jimmy Noy and I recognized him from the description,' but when Simon commanded me, in a flabbergasted and angry voice, to repeat the description, I had to agree with him that that might have fitted any old fisherman thereabouts.

'Oh, I only thought–'

'*What* did you think, Carey?' he asked, on a low note.

'I thought he was helping you because he was a friend of yours and you were doing it to help Lady Isadora,' I said, on a little rush.

'Did you indeed!' he said grimly.

I tried to slew round to look into his face. 'Simon, don't be cross with me,' I begged him.

He softened, and pulled me back against

162

him, and we rode silently, one of the most blissful horse rides, I have ever had.

But nothing had been resolved. Simon hadn't said he hadn't seen the extra candelabra before. He hadn't exactly denied knowledge of it. He hadn't allowed that Jimmy Noy might have been embroiled in the family plot. All he had done was to deny his personal appearance on the night the Candles were filmed for the newspapers, and he had protested that the description Percy had given might have fitted any one of several people, not just old Jimmy Noy.

And I was so much in love with him that rather than stir things up and spoil everything, I let it slide, and didn't try to find out any more. I was contemptuous of myself, because I knew very well that there was nothing in this for me. Simon couldn't marry me. He hadn't said he wanted to, anyway. All he had said was that he loved me very much. Anyway, Sir Hilton had as good as said there was nothing in it for me. I was choked again when I left Simon.

That day the Americans came. They seemed to be in charge of an elderly American with very heavy framed glasses, a slow nasal accent, and a lot of camera equipment hanging on the front of him. He was introduced at Gideon McFee and he talked an awful lot. He introduced the rest of his party. Lady Isadora might well be bored with them as individuals, her eye on the cash they would bring, but I thought they were a very interesting lot. There were two sisters called Dorcas and Dorothea Shorrock, who consulted each other in whispers before they even allowed that the weather was inclement for the time of year; faded of hair, and shrunken of form, their shrivelled faces were belied by wide eyes filled with childlike wonder. 'Since Pa died,' they confided to me, 'and left us everything, we have to make up a lifetime of staying home and being domesticated. We've seen nothing and we wanna see everything, and we just can't go back to the States without seeing a ghost in one of your old haunted houses.'

Miss Leah Adwill, on the other hand, was tough and fifty, brisk and hard as nails, and very sensible. A school teacher, she wanted to go back to her school with as many impressions of English houses as possible, and quite clearly she neither believed in ghosts nor expected to be surprised by one. Her eyes twinkled, making her homely face very likeable as she asked me, right out, 'Tell me, my dear, have you seen this ghost, candles, isn't it?'

Somehow that remark cast an aspersion on me as well as on the family, and I was delighted to say, with dignity, that I was the only one who had seen the apparition on one occasion. That seemed to me to be sticking to the truth and striking a blow for the family's prestige at one and the same time, and it caused something of a sensation. Little Mr Kimble Rolland and his wife Abigail, who were shopkeepers in a small town in the Middle West and pillars of the local church and who had saved all their lives to visit England, had somehow got into this party through striking up a friendship with Gideon McFee on the boat, and they looked as if they wished they hadn't come. The fact that I claimed to have seen something supernatural seemed to make me supernatural in their eyes, but not so in the eyes of the seventh member of the party. He looked tolerantly at the Bergmans, a boy and girl honeymooner, who might have chosen almost anywhere, any company, so lost in themselves were they, but to me he looked anything but tolerant. 'If you've seen a ghost, Miss Carey,' he said, with a wide and good-natured grin that crinkled his good-looking young face up and made it

very likeable indeed in spite of its shrewd-
ness, 'then I'll eat this here hat o' mine and
mighty tough it'd prove to be.'

'Then don't claim to be able to do such a
thing,' I said severely, 'until you've seen our
ghost!'

'Oh,' he drawled, looking down at me
from his six foot two height, 'is it laid on to
order, then?'

'Not that I know of,' I returned, 'but it
certainly seems to me to appear too often
for my comfort.'

'Why d'you stay here, then, or am I kinda
inquisitive?'

'I will tell you, regardless,' I said sweetly. 'I
have no home, I like the family, I enjoy the
work and I feel some loyalty to the family!'
which seemed, for a moment, to leave him
taken aback. I was going to have trouble
with him, I could see!

Still, they were flatteringly pleased with
the rooms allotted to them, in spite of the
fact that Miss Kidby had made a lightning
raid and huge sortie with every maid and
helper she could lay hand on, on the attic to
bring down enough furniture to make the
huge apartments seem comfortable enough
to tempt people like these, who could have
the pick of the coastal hotels. Of course,

their rooms all looked over the beach, which I supposed intrigued them. They would be able to see Simon go riding at five thirty, if they woke at such an hour, I thought sourly. They would also have night winds buffet their windows, straight off the sea, and even our stout stone walls couldn't entirely keep out the sound of the really big breakers crashing in.

From the first, I envisaged the advent of the Americans with apprehension as well as anticipation. Lady Isadora made the whole family attend at meal-times, so Sir Hilton and Mr Rex both rang for me at once and became immersed in work so that they didn't have to entertain the party between meals. My work piles grew, and Lady Isadora said that I should put myself at the disposal of guests too, considering what they were paying for board and lodging.

Miss Kidby was no longer so amiable, because she was so extra busy, and Simon became withdrawn because he hated his accident to be talked about, and the Americans scented it out from the first, somehow, and kept on about it.

Their first day at Wishbourne was the longest day I had ever experienced, and Lady Isadora regretfully admitted the same thing to me just before dinner, when she was giving me an extra list to type out before I set to work on her next speech for the Institute.

'I don't mind the older members of the party so much,' she said crossly, 'but I confess I don't like that young man, that Brett Pilkington, and the way he looks at you. I don't know how you do it, Carey, really I don't, but as soon as a young man steps into this place he starts looking silly at you. I'm terrified that someone will want to marry you and carry you off. Already you've stayed longer than any other clerical help we've had.'

'I don't even like Brett Pilkington,' I said, without thinking.

'That's what you said about Simon,' she reminded me, and then looked rather sorry she had spoken.

And so my mind was on that rather aggravated subject when the news came through of yet another body floating beyond the Point. Sir Hilton told me that it happened every so often, and then the Americans, all sipping their aperitifs, wanted to know about it. Sir Hilton began to explain the movement of the tides, and Mr Rex broke in to correct him, so that it was something of an anti-climax that Lady Isadora came in, heard what they were talking about, and remarked tartly, 'I see you've all found a mutual interest in floating bodies, but this one happens to be one of our local fishermen, which makes it very odd indeed to think of him as a victim to tides he knows like the back of his hand.'

I looked round for Simon, as Lady Isadora explained to the Americans that the drowned man's name was Jimmy Noy.

Chapter Eleven

I remember that night so well. At that time of year the evenings were not famous, weatherwise, for pleasant winds. They roared and whined and made noises rather like those of animals in pain, and thudded against the stone walls in a way that always puzzled me. The guests loved it, of course. They said it gave local colour, and hoped it wouldn't turn out to be just another accidental death. That, they said, would be outside of everything.

Gideon McFee held forth at length. 'Lady Isadora, ma'am,' he said weightily, 'I have to tell you that I have been practically all round the coast of little old England and after giving it a great deal of solid consideration, I have come to the conclusion that for such awful coastlines your coastguards are not trained up to standard. Yes sir!'

I felt sick. All sorts of considerations were jostling in my mind and they didn't concern our much maligned coastguards, who did a sterling job and got little thanks. I was trying to work out when Jimmy Noy could have been last seen.

The Shorrock sisters told each other, with firm conviction, that it was really worth coming to Wishbourne, for here was something happening on their first day, their very first day. Leah Adwill looked thoughtful and asked for the statistics of the drownings beyond the point, and the Rollands said nervously that in their town nobody, not nobody, lost their lives in such a violent way. Their town, they said, was a quiet respectable town. They looked as if they wished they were there at that very moment.

I couldn't tell where Simon was looking. He was hiding behind those dark glasses. I would have to edge out somehow. I wasn't supposed to be there. Sir Hilton had brought me in and said I was to have a drink with the party. I looked out of place, in my working clothes, a fine jersey and pleated skirt. The women of this party were dressed as well, if not with such good taste, as Lady Isadora, and Simon, my own Simon, looked heavenly in dinner dress, clothes so well tailored he appeared to have been poured into them. I was so pleased with him, so proud of him.

But that mind of mine wouldn't let me be

happy for long. I fancied his mouth curled up at one corner. I remembered he had told me that Wishbourne had no connection whatever with smugglers, or pirates or anything so romantic, yet he used the old smugglers' way himself, regularly, apparently! And even as I watched him as he moved over to speak to Mr Rex, he was walking straight towards a small table. I held my breath, waiting for him to knock it over, but he didn't; in spite of those dark glasses and his tricksy sight since the accident, he saw it, and avoided it neatly.

He wasn't in one of his nicer moods tonight. I could tell at once. It was a stranger standing there holding his glass. I wanted to move towards him but the Shorrock sisters buttonholed me to tell me a story which would betray in a well-bred way the fact that they were very rich indeed, a fact which I had guessed from the first. But it didn't stop me listening to everyone else, and I watched Simon's face when someone asked when the man had been drowned, and someone else said it was Monday. Monday, the day that the Candles were seen, the day that the cameraman had been given a lift by Simon. He knew it. His jaw tightened, a little nerve ticked there. I saw him tighten his fingers on the stem of his glass. I wonder it didn't snap.

It was Sir Hilton who actually said it. Everyone looked at each other. The Americans were gleeful, thrilled, all except Brett who was going to worry me. Gideon McFee said, 'Well, what do you know! So it's true! In this family, you give someone a lift, them ole Candles are seen sure as Jackety, and wham, you have a death on your hands!'

The Shorrock sisters told themselves they sure were seeing Life. The Rollands looked distinctly unhappy, but the school teacher looked keen. She said crisply, 'You really believe this little man, this Noy, was a fisherman who lived nearest this estate? Well, I guess he came under the influence of your ghost all right, but don't it make you all feel kinda responsible?' She said it kindly, but shrewdly, and heaven knew the family were looking just that ... responsible, for Jimmy Noy's life. And well they might, when I recalled that Percy had described him, up in our attic, looking as involved in this Candles plot as the rest of the family.

Sir Hilton pulled himself together and said, 'Yes, well, we are jumping to conclusions. There will be an inquest, of course, and we must wait to hear what the coroner will have to say,' which was a master stroke, because

Gideon McFee wanted to know all about a coroner's court and whether the inquest was a thing that could be done without.

Only Simon looked at me, and of course that tiresome, good-looking young man, Brett Pilkington, whose dark hair was impeccably cut and greased just enough to keep every hair in place, and who hadn't a care in the world. His pockets were undoubtedly far from empty, he was free as the air, and he was nobody's fool.

When I slipped out presently, it was to leave the Shorrock sisters boring Lady Isadora to tears, and Miss Adwill crossing a sharpish sword with Mr Rex on his own subject, while Gideon McFee wouldn't let Sir Hilton go, having tied him down to discuss the judiciary system. At any other time, I think the family would have been delighted to have such lively guests, paying guests, that is. But at this moment they had too much on their minds. True, the Bergmans didn't bother anybody. They sat in a corner and smiled into each other's eyes. Briefly I envied them. How nice to have my Simon, my own Simon, the one with the lovely moods, all to myself.

I pulled up sharply, and looked out of one of the windows, my throat all tight and choky again. I must, I really must, stop thinking about that man. As he had told me, pretty firmly, there was nothing in it for me. And as I stared unseeingly, I thought I saw him come round from the garage, in his top coat, running a little to avoid the drops of rain starting to fall.

A voice behind me said, 'Don't you feel you should be downstairs going in to dinner with the others, ma'am?' It was Brett Pilkington, and his smile vanished when he saw I was choking back those ready tears. 'Have I said something? Don't they let their secretaries eat in this country? Or shouldn't I talk with you privately – is that it?'

'Shouldn't *you* be going in to dinner with the others,' I returned. 'Lady Isadora is very particular about the meal starting on time.'

'Oh, I know,' he grinned unrepentantly. 'I told her so at the moment I arrived and I made a sweeping apology for any bad things I might do, me not having been in England before in my life. She understands. She's a great gal.'

'Well, great gal Lady Isadora may well be in your opinion, but in mine she's a fair if martinettish boss, and I shall be for it if I stand gossiping. *You* can do what you like!'

'Dear Simon slipped out. He'll be late too,

so why pick on me?' he drawled, laughing. 'How everyone pampers that fellow! Me, I'd like to give him a poke right on the nose!'

'No!' I said, in alarm. 'No listen, Mr Pilkington, you just be careful of Simon! He's ill.'

'He's *wha-at?*'

'What I mean is, he isn't fit to be in a fight. He's had an accident – didn't they warn you? He had a rock flung at his head, and it's affected his memory, and his sight. Sometimes he walks right into a wall and at others he's all right with the dark glasses.'

'But that's...' he said, murmuring something that sounded like Latin, the name perhaps of Simon's condition. Then he stopped looking baffled, and laughed. 'You're kidding me! Yes, you are! I'm a doctor, and I know what I'm talking about when I tell you that chap hasn't got any such thing.'

'You're a doctor? But no-one said!' I gasped.

'No-one asked me, and when I'm on holiday I do like to stay incognito, otherwise, no holiday for me, on account of everyone discovering they want to tell me about their medical history or treat their sore throats and bunions on the spot. No, ma'am, and you just keep it to yourself.'

'But it's true about Simon,' I insisted. 'I've seen him walk into a wall! Oh, don't let him know, he'd never forgive me for telling anyone. He's so proud and he does hate it so. Please, promise?'

'Okay,' he said slowly, 'I promise. Kinda like this Simon, don't you?' he asked me and looked so searchingly that I could feel the hot colour rushing up my face.

'Of course not!' I repudiated it. 'Well, that's to say, I'm anxious on his behalf, because I'm only staff and he's been very decent to me. At least, some of the time. That's the trouble. He behaves like two men, and he never remembers what he did at those other times.'

He looked at me for a long minute, then suddenly seemed to make up his mind. 'Okay, I'll consider him again,' he promised, and nodding, though still frowning, he turned and strolled back the way he had come.

What had Simon left the company for, in the drawing-room? Had that been Simon I had seen outside? Even allowing for the time lapse, I didn't think it possible. My immediate problem was Brett Pilkington, though. He was going to be a nuisance, one way and another. I wished he hadn't come.

So was the school teacher; she was so shrewd and she wanted to read some of the books in the library. She was always in there and the honeymooners were always underfoot, trying to find a quiet hole in which to hide and be together.

One-ness, the Shorrock sisters said sentimentally but the school teacher promised she would find somewhere for them to go and be alone, so that it wouldn't bother anyone else, at least when the maids were doing their room.

I never thought she'd hit on the attics. That was a great shock when I found them there. I had gone up to go through the little door down to the cave. I could, of course, have simply found the big staircase leading to the attics and slipped through the panelling there but I also wanted to check that both pairs of candelabra were there, one dusty and hanging from the ceiling, the other shining in the darkness of the toy cupboard.

I never saw either, when it came to the point, because the Bergmans made me jump. They were sitting in a close embrace on a settee of the Napoleonic period, covered in a dust-sheet. Tootie Bergman smiled her silly pretty smile and said, 'Hello!' to me, and her husband looked up with a preoccupied frown and said, 'He went thataway!' and pointed down to the other door.

'Who?' I asked.

'What's His Name – Simon. The Lord of the Manor.'

That was him all right, in his present arrogant mood. I said, nervously, 'Did he see you?'

Buddy Bergman said carelessly, 'I dunno. Didn't look up for long enough. Can't tell, what with those dark blinkers of his, anyway.'

I left them to their kissing, feeling rather lonely, and I hurried on to the little stairs.

I was very disconcerted. I had hoped that that way could be kept secret. I said, as an afterthought, over my shoulder, 'Why don't you two go down to the Yellow Sitting-Room? There's nobody there.'

Tootie said, coming up for air, 'Oh, yes, there is. That old school teacher is telling those old fuddy-duddies not to be silly and want to go back to their quiet town because excitement does you good! I'll say it does!'

She went back to her kissing and my last hopes vanished. I went on, reflecting that it must be an unusual state to be in, not to wonder why two people like Simon and his aunt's secretary should want to be going through the attic with such purpose.

I got another shock when I found the door in the panelling. It was open. Surely, surely the careful Simon couldn't have left it open? I was torn between going down there to see who else had discovered it, and going quietly along to listen at each room door and find out who it was by a process of elimination. As I knew where Miss Adwill was, and the Rollands, and the Bergmans, and as I could hear the voices of the Shorrock sisters raised in eager comparison in their own room, it only left the two American men, Mr Rex and Sir Hilton. I didn't think for one moment that it could possibly be Lady Isadora.

I always carried a small torch with me nowadays. Although it was broad daylight outside, the day hadn't got much light in it. We had settled down to some bad weather since the Americans had arrived, although they didn't seem to mind. Their whole existence was geared to 'seeing the ghost' and already copies of the London newspaper in which Percy's account had appeared, littered Wishbourne. Almost every one of the American party had bought up several copies of it to send to the folks back home and to stick into scrapbooks.

Who, then, had been so enthusiastic as to find the secret way? I had shut it behind me. I didn't want anyone else to find out. I crept down the dusty stairs in my stockinged feet and stood there, horrified, as I realized it was the shrewd Brett Pilkington. I might have known he would be the one to pry with the most success and the shortest possible time!

He was standing well back in the shadows, watching something. I manoeuvred until I could get round behind him, see what he was looking at. Finally I was rewarded. It was, of course, Simon, in the well-lit cavern he had fitted up as living quarters, confident that no-one else would know about this except me, and he wouldn't expect me because I had only approached it from the beach and the tide was coming up.

I had to get Brett away. Before he saw too much. But how? So easy to speak to him, ask to know what he thought he was doing. But then Simon would hear us and he would be so angry, and possibly it would do him harm after that accident, to get so angry.

I devised a way of drawing Brett off silently. I threw a piece of small broken stone down so that it just touched his foot and glanced away. I did it from the corner, so that he could just see a movement as I slipped round and out of sight. It wouldn't be in human nature for him not to follow me to see who it was.

I had estimated rightly, but hadn't allowed for a ferocious anger to spill over from Brett. 'I mighta known it was you,' he said, in a bitter undertone, as he caught me within sight of the top of the stairs. 'What are you doing here?'

'I found the door in the panelling open. It's supposed to be a secret,' I told him, equally angrily. 'What are *you* doing here?'

'What I promised you I'd do,' he said, cooling just a little. 'Studying that chap. He baffles me.'

'But how did you find the secret door?'

'Don't punish yourself, honey. I was trailing him and saw him vanish through it. For the son of the house, he sure acts furtive at times.'

'At times,' I repeated, for that was the only thing that really interested me. 'Only at times.'

'You noticed that too!' He brightened. 'Honey, you and I have to talk and I don't fancy that chap coming on us from behind. You might think, in your girlish romantic dream-world, that he's a nice fella, but honey, he's dangerous and don't forget it. Come on!'

I thought of Simon's kisses, and I looked at Brett as if he were the one who was dangerous; dangerously unbalanced to say such a thing. But he took no notice of me. Taking my hand, he chose his moment to get out of the panelling, waiting with nice timing, for Miss Kidby to go by with an armful of clean linen and a housemaid to take a bin in the other direction filled with rubbish from the bedroom bins.

'Now!' he said, and out we went, shutting the panel carefully behind us. 'Get into something warm and waterproof and meet me outside the West Gate, and make it good and quick, honey, because I don't want to collect any stray participants in a country walk.'

I did as he said. It happened to be my free time and Lady Isadora was beginning – since the Americans and their money had arrived – to think I needed some fresh air every day.

Brett looked at me in approval. I had an anorak and slacks and a waterproof head square, mostly brown, and I felt warm and comfortable. He was in a very workmanlike whitish trenchcoat, the collar turned up against the searching wind, and he said bluntly, 'Those shoes fit for a long walk?'

'Haven't got time for a very long walk,' I told him, giving him the exact number of minutes at my disposal. 'I count my free time in minutes because I don't get much of it and I like to enjoy it.'

Brett said, 'You won't enjoy this. I'm going to tell you something you won't like to hear.'

'Not about Simon,' I said quickly, defensively.

'Jeepers, is that the way it is?' he asked, looking upset.

I coloured. 'Not really. There's nothing in it for me. I must be sensible, and find a nice ordinary man who won't mind marrying a foundling, because Simon is due to marry a local heiress. He must.'

Brett grunted. We mounted a bank and dropped down into a lane, cut deep in a fold of the downs. The village was behind us. We had the world to ourselves. Brett turned our faces to climb steadily, leaving the lane behind, and he said, 'If she can be persuaded to. She'd be wise not to.'

'Oh, but why?' I could hear the anguish again in my voice.

'Listen, honey, I told you, I'm a doctor. And you were so wretched about it that the next time I saw the chap, I got talking with him. I gave him a consultation, for free, and it's like I said.'

'Like what? Tell me.'

'I've seen this before. Know anything about the nerves of the eye? No, well, I guess you wouldn't. Let me put it in a simple way, for you. He had a blow on the head. It hurt the optic nerve. It also damaged the part I guess we call the memory. Well, that's over-simplifying it, I guess, but let's put it this way. One day something will go. One way or the other. A loud noise near, or another blow on the head. I've seen it happen.'

'You have?' I couldn't wait to know. 'What happened?'

'The poor guy was stone blind. Couldn't do a thing for him.'

I considered it, my heart crying out so loud, he must have heard. Anyway, for one reason or another, he took my upper arm and held it in a firm grip as we climbed higher. The sea lay below us, for some reason a brilliant blue. The sky, so dark earlier, had now cleared, and though it was still cold, the sky was a bright unnatural blue, and it all had the quality of ice. There was ice round my heart. I said, 'What else?' and he said, because he was a frank, and I think, honest young man, and knew I wouldn't want prevarication, 'I guess he wasn't much good in the head, either, after that.'

'Oh, no!' I gasped.

He slid his arm down, round my waist, and gripped me tight as we walked. 'I said, Carey, that that was what happened to this chap I knew. It could have gone the other way. Remember that.'

It was scant comfort but I thanked him for it.

'There's another thing,' he said. 'I suppose there just wouldn't be a doctor or a nurse in the family, or some friend who could have talked about this?'

I said I thought not, puzzled. 'Why?'

'I dunno. I guess I'm looking for things that don't exist. What was the guy doing down there in that cave, anyway, that you were so anxious for me not to see?'

'Pacing. Counting the paces.'

'Good grief, why? For Pete's sake!'

'He believes there's gold there and he exists only to find it,' I said. 'Don't look so staggered. The whole family know about the legend but they don't all believe it. I don't understand it but they seem to think Simon doesn't believe it. Lady Isadora looked very peculiar when I told her he did.

She said he didn't.'

'How come you knew about that place? Did he tell you?'

'He showed me how to get in from the shore, but it was Percy – the reporter, you know – who discovered the way in from the house. He showed me.'

'I don't remember any mention of buried treasure and secret passages in the news-paper article.'

'Well, it was primarily about the ghost, you see. Besides, I did ask him not to betray it. Simon didn't want it to get around.'

'And he didn't betray it!'

'Well, he was a decent young man, Percy. I quite liked him,' I said defensively.

Brett didn't answer that. He said instead, 'This ghost business, Carey, do you really believe you saw something supernatural?'

'Oh, I wish you hadn't asked me that,' I cried. 'You see, I don't know. Simon spoke about it when I first arrived. He gave me a lift from the station–'

'He did?'

'Yes, and he seemed rather facetious, but the chauffeur was very anxious and scared, and he died later. It was his death, the first time I saw the Candles.'

'You really saw a ghost of Candles, Carey?'

187

'Brett, I don't know. I don't know. I only know that they were transparent. I could see the suit of armour right through them, and there was no trace of candle-grease, and now I come to remember it, no smell of candles burning or being put out.'

'You're trying to argue against it being rigged, you know,' he said, with a sidelong glance at me.

'I know I am because so many people are sceptical and Simon, in some moods, isn't at all facetious and seems to be angry. All the family are angry. I think they're trying not to believe it is something they don't understand.'

'How did the Candles go in the end, I mean? Just ... vanish? Or fade? Or what?' he asked thoughtfully, so I had to tell him I hadn't seen them go, because of my attention being caught elsewhere.

'And where was Simon while all this was going on?'

'He was there, within sight. He was looking at me. Funny, I don't remember him running into anything that night. It's queer, you know. Sometimes he doesn't. He ran slap into a wall once. I told you before – I'm sorry to repeat myself! He won't thank me for telling you. And sometimes his eyes look peculiar.'

'That's what I was trying to tell you, I guess. Peculiar, well, yes, I guess they do.'

And then he said, before I could say it myself, 'But he didn't run into that coffee table that first night we were there, having drinks. I looked at you. You were just longing to run and warn him, only like the good girl you are, you didn't. You just stood still and prayed. And he didn't do it.'

'No, he didn't run into it,' I agreed.

'In fact,' Brett said, very thoughtfully indeed, 'for a chap with what he's got, and eyes like his, he did a very nifty job of avoiding that coffee table, now I come to think of it.'

Chapter Twelve

'He isn't pretending, Brett,' I said quickly. That was the only thing I could think of. Brett thought Simon was acting a part.

Brett looked at me.

I added, for good measure, 'I've seen the scar, you know. Lady Isadora made him show it, though once before when I asked to see it, he wouldn't show me. He got very angry.'

Brett didn't answer for the moment. Finally, he said, 'I too have seen the scar.'

I was so absurdly pleased. 'Well, then!' I said. But he wasn't satisfied. He didn't exactly say it didn't prove anything, but I felt that was what he was thinking and I didn't understand why.

'I want to see your ghost, Carey,' he said suddenly.

I laughed. 'So do the rest of your party!'

'I didn't mean that,' he said, soberly. 'I meant that I wanted to see it after I had assured myself that the original Candles are where they are supposed to be, covered with dust and cobwebs and hanging from the ceiling of the attic.'

I thought quickly. Wasn't he interested in the others in the toy-cupboard? He said, as if following my line of thought, 'I could arrange with the honeymooners to be up in the attic all the time, though whether they would be conscious enough for keeping warden, or whether they'd be so far away in their own rapture that someone could come and steal any Candles from under their noses, I am not sure.'

'I see what you mean. I've wanted to do that, too.'

'And if I do find they've been rigged, I guess I shall have to come right out and tell the world,' he said firmly.

'Oh, Brett, no! Poor Lady Isadora! Anyway, why will you? You're a doctor – you said so. How does it concern you?'

'Well, I guess,' he said, thinking hard, 'that it is sorta because I'm one of those pests known as an honest man, but mostly,' he added, with a wry but engaging grin, 'on account of my young sister's going to marry old McFee's nephew, so I shall expect to have his flaming Society on my back for the rest of my life and you can bet your sweet life that old McFee will raise Hell if he thinks there's been monkey business.'

'Well, I don't get it!' I exploded. 'I thought I could trust you, or I would never have told you all this.'

'Yes, you would,' he said calmly, 'because your honesty sticks out all over you like the hairs on a burr. Besides, you're torn apart with your loyalty to the family because you think you're stuck on that Simon, and you're not. Baby, you just couldn't be. I have to tell you he's no good.'

'Don't you say that about Simon!' I was trembling with anger, but I had to admit that there were times when I had grave doubts myself. 'He's sick and I'm going to get him well and – and–'

'Just don't cry, Carey, don't cry,' he said quietly. 'I couldn't bear that, and you'd hate me for what I'd do. So just don't do it. Let's be sensible, good and sensible, for heaven's sakes. This family of aristocrats that you British set such a store by, are just a lot of cheap jacks in my opinion. Oh, I don't have a thing against any section in this country or any other. I'm just talking about this one particular family, these Holfords. And I have to tell that we have the same kind of folk back home in the States. Why, I could tell you about one such family, they were so proud and so old, why, they almost committed murder to keep their home and their old name.' He looked hard at me. 'Come to think of it, these Holfords might almost be doing the same thing.'

'Now you're going too far, Dr Pilkington.'

'Dr Pilkington, and it was Brett just now,' he reminded me. 'And who's to say I'm going too far? You tell me. Here we have a ghostly apparition of candelabra which brings a death with it. It's happened twice. Now, if it's a supernatural event, okay. Okay! But if it's rigged, why then, you tell me what you would call those two deaths.'

I hadn't thought of that before. My breath caught in my throat. I swallowed, and said firmly (well, I tried to make it sound firm) 'Accidental death.'

'No, we haven't any such thing as accidental death. That's only what your coroner called them. Me, I'd settle for *rigged* accidental death and that, Carey baby, has got another name, not a pretty one.'

'But Simon wouldn't...' I began.

'He might, if he honestly has what you would have me think he's suffering from. On the other hand, if he's heard about this condition, and thoughtfully gave himself a blow on the head (or persuaded someone else to do it for him), and this self-inflicted wound didn't give him this condition, then it's a fair bet that he's acting a part, and if he's only acting sick in this way, then, Carey baby, he would. Jeepers, he would, if it suited him! For I honestly believe that guy's got nerve, but *nerve!*'

I was crying. I couldn't stop, either. The bottom of my world had dropped out, because I knew that Brett was being reasonable and honest and *right*. But he was saying these things about my Simon and I just couldn't bear it.

He stopped and took me by the shoulders and shook me. 'Don't do it, Carey – I told you!' But it was no use, I just couldn't stop. He said again, 'Don't do it! Well, then, like I said, I'm going to have to take you in my arms, and you won't like it, and I might just disgrace myself too, if you don't stop, and you'll just hate that!'

With my face against his coat, I wrestled with my emotions, and finally, with a gasping breath, I had stemmed the tears. 'I love him so, Brett,' I choked.

'You think you do,' he said, very quietly.

'No, I know I do ... sometimes, and then sometimes I almost hate him. I wish I understood myself.'

He said, his arms still round me. 'Have

you considered finding out, honey, if this guy's got a twin brother? How does that strike you?'

It was meant to shock me, I know, but it had no shock value. I had already thought of that and discarded it. I told him so. 'I even asked Simon if he was a twin, and he said no. He said right out, "I am not a twin." So you see, Brett, that won't work.'

'Just a thought, baby,' and he sounded preoccupied.

'What if he had been a twin?' I asked absently, thinking of how much I had adored Simon in the cellar on those two occasions, and of how much I had hated and feared him in the cave. It ought to mean something, solve a problem, but I couldn't see how.

Brett was getting excited. 'Listen to me, Carey – how does this seem? Say there are two of them – well, the chap I gave the consultation to, he had this condition I've been talking about. I'm sure of it.'

'Then why did you say he hadn't and that he was acting a part?' I took him up swiftly.

'Because he doesn't always react as he ought to. The time he avoided the coffee table, for instance – that ought to have been plumb impossible.'

'Yes, I thought of that,' I agreed.

'And there's this business of not remembering he's seen someone on another occasion, or been in some other place, or giving a lift to someone – your stories, Carey baby, but I believe you.'

'But you said that's consistent with his condition,' I swiftly took him up. He was disappointed. 'I guess I did,' he agreed.

'But there *is* something which puzzles me,' I said, 'though I don't see how it can be so,' and I told him how I thought I had seen Simon coming in out of the rain just before Brett had spoken to me that first night, yet Simon had been down there drinking with them, when he had avoided the coffee table. And there was that other occasion when he had ridden that black horse along the edge of the shore, and then suddenly appeared in the cave. The time factor wasn't always credible. 'Yet it can only mean that there are two of them and it can't be so, it just can't be. He said he wasn't a twin, and I really know that to be so.'

'Because you love him and believe him?' Brett mocked gently.

'Not entirely. Mainly because the others would have said so, and they haven't.'

'Oh, I don't know. I guess they would hide

a thing like that, wouldn't they?' he said slowly. 'Because of the succession to the title? Like royalty and your other English customs?'

'There's no title,' I said.

'Now Carey, that's not so! Sir Hilton?'

'Sir Hilton has no sons, so he can't pass it on. It wouldn't go to Simon because ... oh, this is difficult to explain. The Holfords are on Sir Hilton's mother's side – he got his title from his father so it just doesn't apply to Simon.'

'I follow that,' Brett said gravely. 'Then that won't wash. This Sir Hilton, he's a decent old guy, have you thought of asking him?'

'Asking him! I didn't have to! He told me all about the family once when I was miserable and far from home. He's a sweetie. No, now I come remember, Simon is an "only" – the other young people were his cousins and they're all gone. Sir Hilton told me how they all died. There's only Sir Hilton and Mr Rex, Lady Isadora and Simon left.'

'Well, how come Lady Isadora got a title, then?' Brett was all at sea again. I said with a smile, 'From her late husband. She's a widow.'

'Oh. Guess that washes out all the possible props to my theory,' he allowed. 'Still, I don't care. Would you fall for the proposition of a double?'

'No, I would not, Brett, and neither would you! Why should Simon have a double? No, you don't know – and neither can I think of a reason. I think he's just the one person, very sick.'

I moved away from him, blushing. I had forgotten how I had been leaning on him all this time. He looked regretful but didn't remark on it. He said instead, 'I mean to put it to the test.'

'How?'

'Don't be afraid, Carey. I guess I haven't got it in me to willingly hurt anyone, unless it was in a fair fight, face to face. But I am going to presume that there are two of them, and base my test on that.'

'There can't be two of them,' I said thinking. 'Their clothes – unless they were in it together (and for goodness sake what reason?) then they'd be always wearing different clothes?'

'Like, for instance, you told me that Simon appeared in the attic when you were with that newspaper guy, and you sounded surprised that Simon was wearing a guernsey and soiled jeans, instead of looking like one of your tailor's dummies?'

'You remembered that? I'd forgotten it.'

'And you were surprised to recall that Simon came in out of the rain, into the cave, after riding that horse, and he wasn't wet, not even damp.'

'Well, for goodness sake, how could two of them manage a switch like that?' I exploded.

'I dunno, but I sure am going to have a whale of a time putting it to the test, and you, Carey baby, are not to do anything, but anything, to stand in my way. Oh, don't fret, I guess I won't go so far as to hurt your precious Simon, on account of it would hurt you. I know that!'

'Yes, but what would it all be for? Just to frighten everyone?'

'I don't know, Carey. I only know that back home the newspapers pay one helluva lot of dough for a story and they don't like folks to play games. They might get rough if they caught on that the ghost in the story was rigged. Get me?'

'Yes, I know. I thought about that. And I'll tell you this – they did think they would rig it, but they didn't in the end. I know Lady Isadora didn't because she looked so sick when it happened.'

'Could be one of the others did it. Sir Hilton?'

'Oh, no, I really couldn't see Sir Hilton doing such a thing,' I said, and I meant it. I wasn't going to tell Brett that Sir Hilton had told me that they would all have a go at it if it was necessary. At the time I had refrained from disclosing to Sir Hilton that I didn't consider he was fitted to make a very good job of it. There was no point. Let poor old Sir Hilton keep his illusions.

'Mr Rex is sure a sinister guy – he might,' Brett considered. I laughed that away.

'Mr Rex is much too conventional to lower himself to get up to such capers,' I said severely.

'Then that only leaves one suspect, doesn't it, Carey baby?'

We were going to quarrel if we continued this unprofitable conversation. I said so, so we walked back to Wishbourne in silence. Funny, how I had cried on him, confided to him my love for Simon, and then had fallen out with him. The atmosphere between us was charged with emotion and I was glad to be back at Wishbourne, to change into my working clothes and start on something constructive so that I didn't have to think of the Holfords, their accidental deaths and their beastly apparition.

Lady Isadora seemed rather distracted as

she signed her letters. She said to me, 'Where have you been, Carey?'

I said, rather defensively, 'Out walking, ma'am.'

'Have you been with … Simon?' she continued remorselessly.

'I went out with Dr Pilkington,' I said.

'But was Simon with you? Or did you see him?' she pressed.

When I said flatly I hadn't seen Simon all day she seemed very worried. She offered the information that Gideon McFee had spent most of the day in the library reading up about the Holford ghost and that Miss Kidby was cross because the honeymooners wouldn't come out of the attic where she had some cleaning to give the maids to do.

'I wish that American party hadn't come,' Lady Isadora said, completely forgetting how much she had adored their lovely offer of dollars. Dollars, it seemed, was no longer a magic word.

'Those two old sisters keep walking about in pairs and talking together and I find it distinctly unnerving. Besides, where *is* Simon?'

'If you want him urgently,' I said evenly, 'I'll go and find him. I expect he's out riding.'

'He only goes at five in the morning. You know that,' Lady Isadora said. 'I suppose you have given up your early walks since the Americans came?'

I let that one go. There was no point. She was cross about something and wanted to take it out of someone and I was the nearest and most suitable.

She went on, 'And another thing about those Americans – they keep talking about the Candles. Well, I know the Candles was the superior attraction, but never have I got so tired of the subject before. Not only that, they have discovered that the apparition appears on another sort of occasion. When there's a first quarter moon on the thirteenth of the seventh or some such nonsense. Anyway, they are quite certain that it will appear tonight and they are all going to wait in the dark and sit staring at the table in the hall for it to appear. I think you'd better try and dissuade them, Carey.'

'Did Simon hear them say that?' I asked breathlessly.

'Why do you ask that?'

'I don't know. Did he?'

'So far as I know, he had gone out when the great discovery was made, so for what it is worth, he doesn't know. If he finds a lot of people taking up their stations in the hall late at night he will be so angry.'

'Well, they shouldn't be banking on it if that is the set of numbers, because this isn't July,' I pointed out reasonably.

'Then perhaps it's the thirteenth of the fifth or the third – I can't remember. I know it's an odd number. Very odd,' she said flatly.

She was so anxious, it wasn't like her. Personally I thought it would do no harm if the American party wanted to take part in such nonsense but later on I heard her trying to persuade them to go to bed early. I couldn't think why. Anyway, I had other problems. Mr Rex came to ask me something.

'I hear that Simon is taking an interest in the old legend about the pirate gold,' he said, distastefully. 'Is this true?'

'Sometimes he believes it's there and at others he says it is nonsense,' I said uncomfortably. I didn't like Mr Rex much. He made me feel so acutely conscious of being a girl, an unwanted girl. I much preferred Sir Hilton to be around.

Mr Rex turned down the corner of his mouth. 'Have you been encouraging him to believe in this silly story?' he asked me.

'I'm sorry, sir, but I don't think I know it,'

I said. 'Only that gold is supposed to be hidden somewhere in the cave. Actually Simon thinks it will be in some other place.'

'Well,' he said, looking at the floor as he spoke. 'Every old family seems to have its legend of buried treasure but this one doesn't happen to do us any honour. None of the Holfords admitted to believing it for that reason. It appears that we were pirates and wreckers at one time – well, one of the ancestors. A bad one, of course.'

'Of course,' I said quickly, but the way he was telling the story, he made me want to laugh. 'And I shouldn't dream of telling the American party about it.'

'As they've ransacked the library, I hardly see how it can have eluded them,' he remarked sourly. 'We shall hear soon that the Santa Cecilia was wrecked and robbed all too soon by the ancestor I mentioned, and how does that make Simon look, searching for the gold bullion? Bars of gold, and doubloons. A child's story! See if you can persuade Simon to restrain his enthusiasm until the Americans have departed, if he must spend his days searching like a schoolboy.'

He really was bitter about it! I promised I'd do what I could, but without much hope.

I suspected that Mr Rex's only interest was in keeping the story quiet and that if gold were found, he would be as thrilled as anyone, about it.

'Oh, and by the way,' he came back to add, 'in case you've heard a garbled version of the rocking stone blocking the cave, you had better have the true version. There is a closing device, but not a natural one, I fear.'

'There *is?*' I had never really believed it, but I believed Mr Rex. If he said so, then there was one. 'Do tell me about it.'

He said, 'I have no intention of doing so. But I will warn you not to go down there when the tide is coming in.' Torn between closing the conversation, and telling me enough to warn me, he said painfully, 'In the last century the villagers picked up extra cash by rowing the credulous out at high tide to see the wonder happening, but there was an unpleasant accident and our stretch of shore was banned at high tide. People appear to have forgotten about it. I don't want the memory renewed, or we may find trippers being brought down from nearby resorts and a lot of unpleasant publicity.'

He looked nervously at me. I felt eager. I must have looked eager. He said hastily, 'I believe the newspaper people didn't find out anything about that, is that so?' so I agreed that it was so. Better not let the poor old thing know that Percy found the secret panel for himself, or that Brett Pilkington had already been down and watched Simon's pacing and counting.

I was going along the dark passage to my room when Simon stepped out in front of me. I examined my own feelings as he took me into his arms. It wasn't the one I liked. I stood there, passive, waiting for him to stop kissing me. He did, and tilted my face. 'What is it?' he asked sharply. 'Been warned off me? Is that it?'

'Perhaps,' I said. 'What about your local heiress? She wouldn't like this,' and that drew from him the comment, 'She'll have to put up with it.'

I suppose it was because of that, which confirmed that this was not the Simon I cared about, which prevented me from mentioning what was expected and being prepared for that night. I suppose in my heart I was well aware that if I begged him not to rig the ghost that night, he would, just to show me that he'd do as he pleased, without warning from me. So I said nothing, and waited until he had kissed me as much as he wanted to. Then abruptly he left me.

I went into my room and banged the door, then softly opened it to watch where he was going. He of course made tracks for the attics. Like one who is going to his room, I remembered thinking. It was that in my mind that made me on impulse run along to his room. It was the last door round the bend of the corridor. I knocked sharply on it and scuttled round the corner out of sight. I don't know what I expected, but the door opened. I jumped back out of sight, every nerve screaming out. Simon was in his room, and at the same time going up to the attics.

But my love for him assured me that I didn't know for certain so I peeped round the corner, and my heart sang, I was so glad I had looked to make sure. It wasn't Simon's fair head popping back but the gleaming dark head of Brett Pilkington. He hadn't seen me. He had been looking up the other end of the corridor. I was so thrilled that it wasn't Simon, that I didn't question Brett's presence. I scuttled to the stairs, my heart singing so loud, it almost burst. But what, for heaven's sake, was I singing about? I might have proved that there were not two Simons but I couldn't make otherwise the fact that my own dear Simon fled at times such as this evening, and the other hateful Simon stepped into his skin: a man who could kiss me like that, knowing he was to marry some unsuspecting local heiress because his family were so broke.

It was with no great pleasure that I settled down to work in the library that night. I could hear the subdued murmur of voices as the Americans settled down to watch. I even heard Lady Isadora's voice, as Brett persuaded her to sit with him. Curious, I looked out, just before they put the lights out, and I saw Sir Hilton and Mr Rex there, but significantly not Simon. Not Simon.

I went to the window and looked out at the still night. The slender crescent moon mocked me. I shivered, dreading what was to happen this night. Would the Americans see that the lights went on, and expose the plotter? I wondered how Simon would take the embarrassment. I wondered what he would say to me for not warning him.

Finally I couldn't stand it any longer. I put out the library lights and went out to join the others.

I caught my breath. They had been right, in expecting to see it. There it was, shimmering golden, yet misty, as if tobacco smoke was caught, clouding, round it. The flames of the candles were completely still. Because I had seen this before, I could be critical, take my time looking at it. I had been trying to work out how it was done, if it was faked. Someone covered in black would be holding it, ready to whip it away, I reasoned, but there was no gap in the stem where a black gloved hand might reasonably be. It was bright enough to show that it was intact.

I heard the sharp intake of people's breath, and a little whimper (that would be from the Shorrock sisters, in subdued excitement) but no other sound, and when another sound did come, it shocked everyone. The sharp report of a gun, just as the Candles disappeared.

Chapter Thirteen

There is always pandemonium in total darkness when something has happened. I waited for it, to check the voices. Sir Hilton's – 'what damned fool did that? Put the lights on!' and Lady Isadora: 'Oh, I didn't think it would be like *this!*' Mr Rex growling about paying guests behaving atrociously with private property, and the other Americans all saying their piece. All there, except the honeymooners, and Simon. And then Simon's voice above the rest: 'Fathead, shooting at a ghost! Who did that? You've pipped *me!*'

I let my breath out in quick relief. So he was there, so he had had no part in it. But this time it was different. Instead of a mad bustling to find the bell to ring for servants, the lights all went smartly up, and there was Simon, lying on the ground bleeding profusely and trying to get up, but prevented from it by Brett Pilkington. Simon was as angry as his painful wound would allow him to be, shouting, 'You damned fool, get off me and let me get up!' but all around Simon lay the tricks he had employed to bring off the 'ghost' act.

The Shorrock sisters were perhaps the loudest of all in their sense of being cheated. 'Gee, he's faked it. It's not a ghost at all!' and the others, chiefly Gideon McFee, loud in their anger at him.

Instead of watching Brett help Simon to his feet, I looked round at the others. Sir Hilton looked worried, Mr Rex plainly annoyed, but Lady Isadora just looked horror-stricken. I couldn't think why. Left to himself, Simon was even at this moment making a nice job of laughing it off as a young man's trick, to see if he could fool his guests. Already the Shorrock sisters were going coy and telling him he was a naughty boy, and hoping he wasn't badly hurt.

They didn't seem to be watching me. I just crouched over him, trying to see what damage was done, and my face was all wet, and he was trying to push me off to get up. Lady Isadora was raising her voice angrily at him, because she had suffered a very bad shock, and everyone else was talking at once, about the way he had pulled off such a hoax so neatly.

I'll never forget that moment. I had had a certain amount of training in First Aid and

I had awful visions of a shattered shoulder. He was bleeding so much. I looked at Brett. 'You're a doctor – why don't you do something?' I said fiercely, and I was sobbing. I can hear my sobbing now.

Brett just looked at me. I didn't realise why just then. He said shortly, 'I know I'm a doctor, honey. I have already looked. It's just a flesh wound. And if you'll just quit your tears and get up, I'll have him taken up to his room.'

The tone of his voice was so harsh, it was like striking me across the face. I sat back on my heels, and it seemed so unreal that everyone else was intent on examining the black cloths, a curious black box, and the Candles, and not looking at us at all.

And as I sat back, I saw him ... the other Simon. In the shadows, just behind the suit of armour. There was a door there, into the gun room, and he melted back into it. He had been standing there, quietly, watching me with an intensity that drew my eyes to his. A replica of Simon on the ground, only there was no blood, and he was so white in the face that it was almost as if he were a ghost, too.

I suppose I must have had a bad shock then and it showed. I heard Brett's voice, against the general pandemonium: 'Carey! Put your head down! Don't faint now, girl – I need your help!'

I ducked my head, automatically, but it was swimming. I couldn't think, I couldn't feel. I just did as Brett told me, in that sharp, authoritative voice.

Some servants came with a sheet or something and they put Simon on it, to carry him upstairs. I heard Gideon McFee saying in his loud nasal voice, 'Well, I will say this, I guess if you can't have a real apparition, that was the slickest fake I ever saw!' and the Shorrock sisters twittering about how frightened they were, but what a thrill it gave them. It was at that moment that the school teacher stopped her theorizing and realized what we were doing. 'That boy's hurt!' she said roundly, and that set Lady Isadora off again.

Brett said, 'Ma'am, you don't need to send for your doctor. I am one. But I've no objection, if you want another opinion,' so Lady Isadora kept quiet. I wondered then if she knew. I decided that she must know.

Brett said, 'Come on, Carey, I need your help!' but Lady Isadora said, 'No, I'll come with you, Dr Pilkington. You go and get some brandy or something, child. In fact, we must all have some.' And she gave me a little push. I couldn't help wondering if she had seen the other Simon, and that she knew I wanted to get into the gun-room. I prayed that he would still be there.

I left Sir Hilton rustling up drinks for everyone. They all seemed to have a lot to say to each other, those Americans. But then, why shouldn't they? They were tourists. It was their holiday. Not their worry – ours. And heaven help me, under his bonhomie as the perfect host, poor Sir Hilton looked very worried indeed.

I slid into the gun room. I don't think anyone saw me go. The suit of armour protected me. And there stood Simon.

I went slowly up to him, but I need not have doubted. He held his arms out to me, and without a single word, we clung to each other, in a tight embrace that made my heart hammer, and the thrills that shook me were pleasant ones, not the rather scaring sensation the other Simon always filled me with. And he kissed me. Kissed me in that way, I didn't want it to stop.

'You're … *you*, aren't you?' I choked, idiotically. But he knew what I meant. He knew what I was thinking, without my having to speak, I was sure. We belonged to each other, and we didn't have to say. This was love, as if we'd been welded together at some time in the distant past, and being forced apart, had come together again, naturally, without need of a single word.

Presently he pushed my head back, smoothed my tears away, and looked at me. He wasn't wearing his dark glasses. He said, 'You didn't know, until just now, did you?'

'Yes, I did – at least, I always thought of you as two people, or at least, one person with two moods, and one I didn't like. I thought it was because of the accident. It used to break my heart, when I thought you were in the other mood.'

He didn't like that, because he knew, as I now knew, that it meant the other Simon had been kissing me. I didn't like the thought, either. 'Who is he?' I asked him.

'He's the other Simon. Simon Nicholas,' he said.

'Your cousin! But Sir Hilton said he was dead!' I cried, then I thought about it some more. 'Oh, no, he didn't. He just said they were all gone, and he told me how some of them died. I presumed he meant them all.'

'Yes, we've all presumed too much,' my Simon said. 'I should have told you, when I first suspected.'

'When did you?' I asked him.

'Down there, in the cellars. From what you said. They'd been telling me it was the result of the accident, but then they honestly thought so. Why shouldn't they? They didn't know Nick was back. They never liked Nick as a boy – Aunt Isadora and the uncles, I mean – so I suppose they didn't want to think he was back.'

'But I don't understand – Sir Hilton said he was red-headed, like his mother. He loved her, didn't he?'

'I don't know about that, Carey. But yes, Nick was red, but it isn't difficult to bleach hair. I wonder when he came back?'

I thought I knew that all right. I said, 'I expect it was the night I arrived. Don't you remember the way you looked at me, when I spoke to you, and you said, "Who the blazes are you?"'

He looked shocked. 'No! Did I? My love, I'm sorry, but I was as worried as hell, that night. I hardly knew what I was saying. The doctor had given me his private opinion that I'd lose my sight anyway.'

'Oh, Simon!' I cried, but he shook his head fiercely, and took me into his arms again.

'No, don't cry, my love. Your face

crumples like a baby's and I can't bear it! And we have so little time, just now. Look, you've got to get me to my room, somehow, and I shall have to have the same sort of dressing and sling as he'll have, because I don't want anyone to know just yet. There are things I must do.'

'But you'll vanish and I'll be left with him,' I protested. 'He's in your room! Oh, that's funny – when he went up to the attics earlier I went to your room (I had the idea there might have been two of you then) but when I knocked and hid, it wasn't you who opened the door, it was Dr Pilkington. What was he doing in your room?'

'Talking to me,' Simon said, ruefully smiling. 'No, he doesn't know there are two of us … yet. But I think he suspects.' He kissed me again and tore himself away. 'I must go, Carey. Now look, I want you to slip out and join the others, and faint or do something outrageous, to give me time to get out and slip under the stairs. That's all I need. Will you do that?'

'Where will I see you?' I asked, clinging to him.

'I'll come and knock at your door, after everyone's in bed, and we'll come down here and talk. Now, off you go. Good girl.'

I really did the job in grand style. The others were still examining Nick's paraphernalia for producing the apparition, and I went among them quietly, and got round the other side of them. They had just come to the end of their explanations for the benefit of the honeymoon couple who, of course, had not been there at the time. All the tourists were very happy to have the opportunity to explain all over again how it was done, and in the middle of it, I was able to collapse in an untidy heap. On the ground. Everyone swooped over me, just as people do when they've never been called upon to help with a fainting person before. It was as well that Sir Hilton and Mr Rex weren't present. They unfailingly made for the drinks table, believing brandy cured all ills. It was as well, too, that Brett Pilkington wasn't there – his bracing tongue pulled one round alone! And a fake faint would have merely angered him.

As it was, the honeymooners gaped, and Tootie started to cry and needed comforting. The school teacher acted with common sense, of course – she would! The horrible Shorrock sisters pushed evil over-powering smelling salts under my nose, and Gideon McFee said I had no stamina and should be sent home to my parents. 'Gal like that is no fit person to be in a haunted house, for I guess that there *is* a real ghost hereabouts somewheres. Kinda feel it in my bones. Sure do wanna stay till we see it.'

The others surprisingly assured him that they wanted to stay too, which surprised me. I decided to come round, and join in this interesting conversation, and I accepted the brandy the school teacher had had the forethought to find, and listened with respect to the tourists. They were not quite as credulous as I had at first thought.

'Lady Isadora,' he said, 'hinted that it might be a fake tonight and we took bets that we'd know how it was done, and we lost and she's the richer for a hundred dollars from me,' he said. And the others disclosed how much they, too, had lost to Lady Isadora. I privately handed it to her that she was a good hand at making money in an engaging way, and I just couldn't think how she dared.

'But that boy, he's taken a cracking,' Gideon McFee went on. 'What with that accident of his and now this – well, Pilkington told me himself that it only wanted an explosion or something, to blow the whole thing sky high.'

'What *do* you mean?' the Shorrock sisters asked, together as usual. 'Send him crazy?'

'Maybe. Maybe blind.' Gideon McFee had his facts right.

Then the honeymooners absolutely stunned me by breaking into the conversation. Buddy said succinctly, 'Which one?'

My heart lurched. I didn't think I'd heard aright. Everyone turned on him and Gideon said kindly, with a tolerance for the lunatic state that young marrieds get into, 'Guess I don't follow you, son?'

'Guess there are two of 'em,' Buddy said stolidly. 'Maybe the one who was shot wasn't the one with the bash on the head!'

He and his little wife both looked at me then, and Tootie said, 'Carey will know which is which. I've seen her kissing them. A girl can always tell by the way a fella kisses.'

Poor Gideon, who had probably never kissed a girl in his life, was for the moment quite put out. He sought guidance from the school teacher, who looked very fierce, because she, too, had probably never had the opportunity of making any such comparison. The Shorrock sisters said that their kissing days were too far in the past to remember anything that would be helpful, so everyone looked at me.

I mustered my wandering wits, and asked Buddy, 'How did you come to think that Simon was two people?'

Buddy said succinctly, 'Know he is. Frightened Tootie in the attic – while I'd gone down to the fridge for double deckers. We get hungry, kinda,' he explained for everyone's benefit. 'Landed the guy a facer, and he skiddaddled down the end of the attic. Then another guy comes up and it's him again only I guess it isn't.'

Tootie said, 'It was him all right. The other one, I mean. The one with the kinda sweet mouth.'

'Oh, shucks!' Buddy said, to that. His new wife wasn't supposed to be interested in such things. 'This other guy come up and he didn't seem to know a thing about it, and he sure did oughta have had a real prize bruise where I pipped him one, but he didn't. No, *sir!*'

'You were mistaken,' I said quickly. Simon didn't want this to get out, and here they all were, eagerly trying to discover when and where they had come to the conclusion that there were twins of Simon. 'I can assure you, Simon isn't a twin! But he does play tricks on people – like tonight! In the attic, Buddy, it was possible for him to have gone down

one staircase and hurried up the spiral staircase to give you a scare.'

'And changed his clothes on the way?'
Buddy said scathingly. 'I maybe forgot to
mention that the guy I hit was in old duds
and the other one looked like a tailor's
dummy, not a speck on him.'

They had me there. Everyone looked to me
for enlightenment. I shook my head, desperately. 'As Tootie says, I should know,' I
pointed out, and smiled tolerantly at the
honeymooners, hoping devoutly that the
other people would think they had been too
bemused with each other, as usual, to expect
to have any credence placed on their words.

But I should have known that the first
glitter of the honeymoon was beginning to
wear off, and Buddy was not the sort of boy
to like having his word doubted. 'I'll show
you,' he gritted at me. 'I'll prove to you that
there are two guys named Simon and I
don't like either of 'em.'

I had no more time to try and repair the
damage. Lady Isadora sent for me. It was
getting late, anyway, and the others were
drifting, very reluctantly, to bed. The butler
had born off the candelabra and all the
other things which Nick had used, and
something had been done about the blood

stain on the flagged floor. Order had been restored, and the servants were patiently waiting to lock up. Wishbourne wanted to settle down for the night, and to my over-wrought imagination, it seemed to me that the grey old house was crouching, angrily – intent on punishing those who had tried to make game of her secrets. Not that Nick cared. I was quite sure it would take more than such an idea to frighten him.

As Lady Isadora pointed out to me. 'You know, child?' she said tiredly, pointing to an armchair by her own, in front of the glowing fire. 'I hadn't meant it to be like that.'

'How had you meant it to be, ma'am?' I asked quietly.

She frowned. 'Oh, dear, I have to tell you everything, I suppose,' she sighed. 'No Hol-ford likes to own up to his grubby little schemes. Oh, well! Gambling is – or used to be – our besetting sin. Neither Hilton nor Rex have it, but I have. Mine were gambling debts, and that was what the threatening letter was about, until I paid up. But now, of course, the story of the fake ghost has come out, and I suppose I shall have to refund to the newspaper. We are not dishonest.'

'Is it as easy as that, ma'am? I mean, they have misled their readers, haven't they?'

'Reporting what they actually saw? I think not.' She smiled. 'Your Percy was clever. He never said he saw a ghost here, remember. Never mind, I have found another profitable source of income, and a quite dignified one, if my nephew hasn't ruined everything.'

She frowned, and I waited, breathlessly. She continued, 'I will tell you what tonight was supposed to mean, so that if the tourists add a little too much colour to their version you will be able to compare notes. It seems that Gideon McFee has not had much luck with actual proof of haunting in old English houses, for his beloved Society, so he thought it might be better to attack the subject from the other way, and try to discover what were the fake hauntings. He is astonished at the way we managed ours and is quite sure he won't be taken in again – on behalf of his Society, of course.'

Now she was laughing, silently, enjoying it all. 'And to add spice – incorrigible spice! – to it, we agreed to take bets. I won, because he just couldn't think how it was done, or even be sure it wasn't the real thing.'

'Might I ask how it was done, ma'am? I don't appreciate the significance of the black box.'

'The black box contains the phosphorus-coated candelabra, and a sliding front comes down sharply to account for the "vanishing" – one mustn't have the smell of the wicks being extinguished, nor risk fire by throwing a black cloth over the whole thing. Nor indeed to break the line of the candelabra's stem by a black hand clutching it. There was a handle underneath the box, to hold it. At the crucial moment, we have to have a commotion to distract people's eyes off the actual "vanishing".'

'Oh, Lady Isadora, you did that, the first time I saw the Candles,' I said reproachfully.

She smiled ruefully. 'I seem to remember it was the new housemaid going into strong hysterics,' she remarked, 'and if I know anything of that girl, she was merely doing it at the instigation of my nephew.'

'Not Simon!' I couldn't keep it back.

She said, 'You know, then. When did you know?'

I shook my head. 'I can't say. It's been coming on for some time. I did ask him if he was a twin and he said no, he wasn't. He was quite firm about it and of course it was true. Oh, no, that wouldn't have been Simon – that would have been Nick,' I said, thinking.

She was looking strangely at me. 'Which

225

one do you love?' she asked harshly. I believe she was afraid for me.

'Not Nick,' I said quickly. 'Simon! *Simon!*'

'And can you tell the difference?' she asked sceptically.

'Oh, yes, I can tell,' I said sadly. 'Nick is the one I always thought was Simon in a bad mood, from the accident, do you see.'

'Yes,' she said, 'I see.'

'Lady Isadora, why did those two men die?' I breathed.

'What do *you* think?' she thrust at me.

'Jimmy Noy was helping Simon (no, Nick) with the painting of the spare candelabra. But Jimmy Noy liked Simon – he let him tether the black horse there.'

'Who else knows about this?' she asked sharply.

'I'm afraid they're all guessing,' I said, and I briefly told her what the tourists had learned from the honeymooners. 'I did my best to persuade them they were mistaken and that there weren't two of them but Buddy Bergman is convinced. So is his little wife. Silly of Nick to do that,' I mused.

'But how like him,' she muttered, suddenly ageing. 'Be careful, Carey. Don't let Nick know you've found out. You've been a good girl with your work. You've blended in with us. I wouldn't like you to be ... hurt.'

'As Jimmy Noy and the chauffeur were hurt?' I breathed.

She nodded. 'Or as Simon was hurt. I'm only guessing, mind, in all three instances. I could be wrong.'

Faithful to the family to the last! I agreed with her, and said quickly, 'How did you know that one of them was Nick, ma'am?'

'How did *you* know?' she countered.

'Little Tootie Bergman says...' I began, then broke off, going rather pink. Lady Isadora nodded.

'Yes. She would. A woman in love. That, of course, was not likely to be my way of finding out. No, you gave me the clue. The occasion on which you said roundly that sometimes Simon said there was gold to be found, and sometimes he didn't think so. Only I could know that it was Nick who always insisted on the gold being there somewhere – he always believed that. Simon, never! Simon shared my view that if ever there was gold hidden, someone would have found it, since that ancient time. This family has always been hard up from gambling, or drinking. No, if one of them was searching for the gold, that meant that Nick was back. It also meant that Nick was wandering about among us when Simon was out. That was always a favourite trick of Nick's. Only this time there was the accident to cloud the issue. We thought it was merely the result of that. We never dreamed of Nick returning.'

'The night I came. And the chauffeur must have guessed.'

When I left her, she looked most unhappy, and well she might. I felt so sorry for her. But I had to go. I couldn't think what would happen if Simon had gone to my room door and knocked and found I wasn't there. It was in the servant's quarters. Difficult enough as it was.

Miss Kidby was going along the corridor. She stopped to speak to me. 'How are you now, miss? I heard you had fainted down there, and well you might, that tiresome Mr Simon doing that awful thing. Still, the tourists loved it, so I suppose we mustn't be too hard on him.'

I assured her I was all right now, and thanked her.

'You don't look too good, come to think of it, my dear,' she said in concern, and she couldn't be blamed for not knowing that my pallor was springing entirely from excitement. 'I think I'll pop along to my room and get you some aspirin. You get into bed and

I'll bring you a hot water bottle.'

I tried to dissuade her but she was adamant. So I went into my room with a new puzzle – what to do if Simon knocked and found Miss Kidby as well as me.

Two hands went over my mouth from the darkness, and the scream that rose in my throat was stillborn, because I knew it was my Simon. How, I wonder? He was masking my mouth pretty firmly, and holding me tightly so that I didn't get away, to run and scream with terror at finding someone in the darkness of my room. Yet I knew it was him by his very touch.

He shut the door and put on the light. 'Sorry, my love, but I couldn't risk anything. Where can I hide when old Kidby comes back?' and when I indicated the wardrobe, he kissed me, like a man who has been waiting years to do just that.

I pushed him away. 'What is it, my love?' he asked, in surprise, but even he heard Miss Kidby's heavy tread, and let me hide him in the wardrobe.

I thought I should never get rid of her, and I couldn't evade taking the aspirin. She stood over me, like a child's nanny, until I did. Then she insisted that I undress, so that she could tuck me in, and she did that, too.

I fumed, but could do nothing, without risking arousing her suspicions. At last she was satisfied, and went.

I put on the light, and told Simon not to come out till I dressed again, but he did. 'Dress behind this screen, and let's talk meanwhile,' he said, 'because there isn't much time. Remember what happens whenever the Candles are seen.'

I was shocked. 'Oh, I know, but this was a hoax and everyone knew it,' I protested, 'so there won't have to be–' and I broke off, because it really was a terrible thought.

'Nick was responsible for those two deaths,' Simon said remorselessly, 'and he isn't going to pull back now.' He stared at me over the top of the screen. 'Carey,' he said suddenly, 'who am I? Simon or Nick?'

'Don't be silly,' I said. 'You're Simon, of course.'

'How can you be sure? Don't say the scar. Nick has one, as well. Make-up. It's easy. For all you know, I might be Nick, and Simon lying cosily in his bed with a flesh wound that bled a bit, and is therefore getting all the attention from the women. Think now – would your precious Simon come and hide in your room?'

I hesitated, but only for a moment. 'You

kissed me. Nick doesn't kiss me like that,' I said. It was only meant for proof, but I could see I shouldn't have done that. Simon was no different to any other young man. He was as jealous as the rest. So I said for good measure, having done the damage, 'Besides, if you had been Nick and not Simon, I doubt if I'd have been allowed to dress decently behind a screen – if at all!'

Naked hatred of his cousin stood in Simon's face for a moment. He had whitened, and I suddenly remembered that I shouldn't upset him, because of that blow on the head. Then I remembered what I should have thought of before, and I said shortly, 'It makes no difference what you think or what I think, or whether you're Simon or Nick. The fact still stands that Simon Holford is engaged to a local heiress, and that I couldn't marry him even if he asked me to, because I'm a foundling and in case you've forgotten the implications of that, just ask yourself what Lady Isadora's views on such a person would be.'

'She likes you. She told me so,' he said in a voice muffled with rage and frustration. 'Besides, I am not now going to marry the heiress or anyone else. I couldn't, now there's you, Carey.'

'You don't listen to me! I don't know who my parents were or whether I have a right to a name at all. Don't you understand?'

'It doesn't matter,' he said. 'Ancestors of ours have been born the wrong side of the blanket–'

'But one half was pure Holford,' I said fiercely, 'and maybe I haven't any decent blood in me at all.'

'Then I'll find out,' he said implacably, 'and until we know, let's not think any more about it. I love you, Carey, do you hear. Only you.'

I had to let him kiss me again then, but not for long. He pushed me away, this time. He wanted to know how many times Nick had kissed me, when and where.

'Now look,' I pleaded, but he would hear no excuses. He wanted to know, so I told him, baldly, and we compared notes and I found out for sure some things I couldn't be certain about. It was my Simon who had me up before him on the horse, but Nick who almost rode me down that first day – it would be! Jimmy Noy hadn't wanted Simon to know who had ridden his horse. There had been high words between them. 'But a worse quarrel between Jimmy Noy and Nick,' Simon said coldly, as he caught my

232

look of anguish. 'I did not kill Jimmy Noy. That would be Cousin Nick.'

'Just because of a quarrel?' I couldn't believe it. 'And don't tell me he did it just because he needed a death to make the legend seem to be coming true, Simon!'

'He did it because Jimmy Noy was blackmailing him,' Simon said simply. 'Remember, Nick wouldn't want the family to know he was living rough, either in Noy's cottage or in the cave.'

'The Cave of Gold,' I whispered, with a shiver. 'Of course, the supplies, in that wooden chest – everything for someone to live there. And he could come up to the attics at night and sleep up there, if he wanted extra warmth.'

'Which I've no doubt he did, until the honeymooners came,' Simon said.

'But it was you with me each time I was burning in the cellar,' I pleaded, and he nodded. 'And it would have been you that Brett Pilkington talked to–?' and he nodded again.

'And Nick who annoyed Tootie Bergman and made her husband hit him!' But Simon hadn't heard about that. I had to tell him all about it, and of course, as I had guessed, and they had, too, it really hadn't been Nick coming up the stairs again. It had been Simon, and he had forgotten that the young people went to the attics for privacy when the maids were doing out their room.

Simon swore under his breath, about the honeymooners. 'Why can't they go out and get some good fresh air? I was looking for the second set of candelabra.' He thought about it. 'Well, if that's how it is, the secret will soon be out, so I suggest that you and I go to my Aunt Isadora and tell her we want to–'

'No, Simon! No! She'd never forgive me. She knows I care for you. She guessed. But she trusts me not to want to do anything about it. Simon, they're broke. They want to keep Wishbourne. There's only one way to do it for them. Don't you want to keep Wishbourne?'

'Not particularly,' he said. 'I want *you*. As to my aunt and my uncles, they need not have got into this financial state, if they'd had a bit of self-control, and eased up on the gambling and the brandy. But that's the Holford family – they were smuggling and wrecking three hundred years ago and I've no doubt they carried on their villainy in every century since, to pull in more cash. Well, I'm tired of it. I was brought up in the tradition, but I want to break free.'

I looked hard at him. 'You don't, you know. You want your cake and eat it. You want the family and the traditions of Wishbourne, and me, too, and nobody ever gets everything they want, Simon. Besides, what about–' and I broke off, biting my lip. No need to remind him about the result of that tragic accident.

'Of course,' he said, very quietly indeed, 'I could remind you that I might go blind, or something much worse, and plead with you to give me a little happiness while there's time, but I won't.'

'Don't!' I choked, and I gave him a push. 'Please go, Simon. I can't bear it. Oh, where will you sleep, though, now Nick's in your room?'

He grinned suddenly. 'On the couch in the attic. Lend me a blanket, love?'

I gave him my warmest blanket, and I hated to let him go. His arms were so comforting, and I clung to him tighter than perhaps I should have done, remembering what Dr Pilkington had said about that other case like Simon's. He was my Simon and he loved me and I loved him, but I didn't think he had much chance. His eyes had that odd look in them again. I said, 'Do you have to go up to the attics?' I was afraid he might trip over something, like the time he had run into the wall.

He let his arms drop to his sides. 'I trust,' he said coldly, 'that you're not inviting me to stay in this room, Carey?'

'No, no, I didn't mean – I don't know what I meant,' I choked, because knowing him and how proud he was, I dare not voice my fears.

I let him go then, and I was just turning back to my bed when a soft scratching on the door broke the stillness of the small hours. It was Simon back again, I thought, and flew to the door.

My face fell, as I saw Brett Pilkington, fully dressed, standing there. He took in, in one swift glance, the fact that I was dressed. He said, 'Oh, not in bed yet. Then I shan't feel so bad about asking you to step down to the cellars. Something quite important I want you to see.'

Chapter Fourteen

I hesitated. I didn't think for one moment that he'd take me on a wild goose chase, not Brett. But I couldn't be sure.

He said, 'I know it's a funny thing to ask in the small hours, but I need help. It's the housemaid, the one who had hysterics – remember? You told me about it – the first time you saw the Candles.'

I said, with a dropping jaw, 'She's … dead?'

'I see you catch on quick, Carey baby. No, not quite. I took her up to the library and patched her up. I don't want to rouse the house. I thought of you. Coming?'

I nodded.

'Good girl,' he approved. 'Put on something warm. It's cold downstairs.'

I could only think of my anorak. It certainly kept the chill of Wishbourne in the small hours, from my bones.

I followed Brett Pilkington's torch down endless corridors, from the servants' floor to the main bedrooms, down to the reception rooms, the hall where the Candles had been so disastrously seen tonight, and still further down, to the place where I had been burning papers.

'What are we coming down here for?' I asked suspiciously. 'You said she was in the library.'

'She'll do for the moment. I want to show you what happened to her,' he said. It was as well he had that powerful torch. He led the way down dark narrow stone steps. Wishbourne wasn't unlike any other house of its age and kind; the part reserved for family and friends being large and spacious and grand, the part for the staff poky and dark and in places dangerous.

'Mind how you go,' Brett warned me. 'She didn't, by the way.'

'What happened? Where did you find her?' I gasped, as he opened the door to the place where I had been burning papers for Lady Isadora. He snapped on the lights, but even with all of them on, the naked bulbs were so low-powered, it was very gloomy indeed. He shone his torch beam to the steps, and there was the remains of a trip-wire.

'But ... I don't understand,' I said blankly.

'Don't you?' He seemed wryly amused. 'Your boy-friend wanted to stage an apparition tonight because he had to get rid of someone. The housemaid. He fixed up her demise first, expecting that while everyone was busy talking their heads off about the "ghost" they thought they had seen, he could go down and take away his trip-wire. But he was prevented, wasn't he?'

'By you shooting him,' I gasped.

'Don't be a goop, Carey,' he advised. 'I am not trigger happy. I was not shooting at him. I shot at the Candles, hoping to dislodge some contraption, to expose it as a fake. I winged my man, that's all.'

'But what made you look here for her?' I gasped.

'I didn't,' he said frankly. 'I had wanted to look round the cellars for some time and tonight was the first opportunity. It was as well I did. I found our little friend wasn't dead–'

'But why should her helping him earn her death at his hands?'

'You don't know the girl? Neither do I but I guess she could make herself kinda tiresome to a guy if she wanted to. Your boy-friend had no patience. A Bad Man, Carey, baby.'

'Don't keep calling him my boy-friend. He isn't. He isn't Simon, not the one with the blow, that you examined.'

'Well, what kinda doctor d'you think I am, not to know that?' he drawled. I felt the colour rising to my cheeks. 'And what kind of a guy do you think I am that I didn't see stars in your eyes when you thought my knocking on your door meant him?'

'Well, you're wrong,' I flared. 'What kind of a girl do you think I am, to expect someone to come to my room in the small hours? And what kind of a man do you think Simon is?'

'A sick man,' he said quietly, 'with a chance of recovery, but a very slim chance. I didn't pull any punches, and he wanted to know the truth.'

I grabbed my middle. It hurt there, as if he had dealt me a body blow. Simon was going to die, I knew it, I told myself, and I might as well be dead, too.

'So you know about the two of them,' I said. 'I hope you're satisfied – I suppose you've left Nick in Simon's bed, where he can get around and do what mischief he likes.'

He looked sharply at me. 'No, he's asleep. He's lost a lot of blood,' he said severely.

'That man has nine lives,' I said scathingly. 'He pops up where you least expect him, and if you were to go up now, I bet you wouldn't find him in his bed.'

'The housemaid,' Brett muttered unaccountably, and turned and ran out of the cellar. I followed him. We left all the lights on and the trip-wire and everything. But of course, when we reached the library, there was nobody there. If the housemaid had ever been there, there was no evidence.

I think Brett had expected it, when I had said that. He looked very angry indeed. 'Guess we should have come here first, but I wanted you to see,' and he tore his hands through his hair.

'But who could have carried her out?' I whispered. 'Nick?'

Brett was thinking. 'She could have walked. She wasn't in too bad shape. I wonder ... if she went up to his room, guessing he was responsible? Let's go, Carey. No, you go back to your room,' he said, on second thoughts.

'No, I'm coming with you,' and I said, 'I must! If Nick isn't there – don't you understand? Simon's asleep on the couch in the attic.'

'And?' There was an edge to Brett's voice. At this moment he wasn't concerned with Simon, but with a girl who now knew that Nick had tried to kill her. She wouldn't be safe.

We couldn't get in Simon's room. The door was locked. Brett looked at me in frustration. 'We'll have to arouse the house,' he said, but I said, 'No. Let's go to the attics and see if Simon's all right.'

Brett hesitated, then said, 'Okay, let's go, but be quiet.'

He knew his way about Wishbourne better than I thought he did. He was quiet, too. I wondered what Simon would have to say to this night's work, and I knew he wouldn't like it. He wouldn't like me being around alone with a personable young man like Brett Pilkington, in the small hours.

Simon was on the couch, with my blanket over him. Fast asleep, with the deep breathing of exhaustion. Brett's face eased, and he looked enquiringly at me. I said softly, 'No, don't wake him.'

Brett suddenly made an exclamation. 'What did we come up here for?' he whispered. 'That wretched girl will be in Nick's room. That was why the door was locked. Come on, or we may be too late.'

I hesitated, looking at Simon's face, but Brett removed the torch beam and I couldn't see Simon any more. I followed Brett. 'What will you do? You haven't got a key!'

'You'll have to go and wake Miss Kidby

242

and ask her for it. Say Dr Pilkington wants to see his patient but some fool has locked the door. I'll go back and listen. Bring it to me!'

He was beside himself with impatience for his own mis-thinking, and what that locked door might mean. I turned back to Miss Kidby's end of the corridor, feeling my way along in the dark. Brett had the torch. This was no use, I thought. I'd never find it. Better to feel my way back my own room and get my own torch.

This I did. It took me considerably less time than fumbling down to the end of the corridor. I looked at the clock and saw that it was almost three. No wonder Simon had been flat out! So was I – how I longed for bed. But there was that housemaid in danger, and if there was one more 'accidental' death at Wishbourne, what would be said?

I closed my door carefully, and was just going to turn right when my torch beam picked out a fold of paper. I picked it up. It was from Simon. *Carey, my love, don't listen to B.P. Dangerous. Forgot to tell you. Come up to me – will explain.* I didn't know Simon's hand-writing, and I could only suppose that he had pushed that under my door after I had gone downstairs, and then had fallen asleep waiting for me. Poor Simon, he had been going to sleep on his feet, I thought, as I abandoned the idea of waking Miss Kidby and hurried up to the attics again.

I shut the door and said, 'Here I am,' and pointed my torch to the couch, but it was empty. My blanket was flung back, and warm to the touch, but he wasn't here. I felt that there was someone in the darkness with me but I couldn't see him. 'Simon, where are you?' I called, and right at the end, I heard his voice, softly: 'Don't shout – this way. Come on!'

'Simon, wait – where are you going? Wait for me,' I called, but he merely called back, 'Come on – want to show you something. Buck up before Pilkington starts looking for you!'

I had no reason to believe then that it wasn't Simon. I didn't entirely trust Brett, I was shocked to find, but I did trust Simon implicitly, and I followed. I didn't even ask myself why someone like Simon shouldn't wait for me, courteously. There was nothing so pressing that he couldn't wait for me, but I didn't think that then. I just blindly obeyed him. Down the wide stairs, round and into the secret panel, and down the cold, cold stone steps to the Cave. If I had any doubts then, I didn't stop to think of them.

'Put that light out,' he called, so I did.

It was not exactly dark, light enough to see the steps by the torch he directed up. 'Battery's going,' he said. 'But it's enough.'

'I've got mine,' I said, but he snapped. 'We don't want much light. Pilkington's around,' so I didn't put it on. I followed him.

He led me down towards the mouth of the cave. People who don't live by the sea rarely bother to keep an eye on the tide chart. It was with a shock that I heard the sea thundering somewhere near. I had never been at this end of the beach when the tide had been high. It sounded rough, and much too near. I said so.

'Well, of course – it's coming up. That's what I wanted to show you,' he explained, over his shoulder. 'You know all that rot that's been talked about a rocking stone? Well, it's no such thing. It's a hand-made mechanism. I've found it, from an old book in the library. Look, here's the lever.'

I was as fascinated as he was. He showed me how he had oiled it, and got it to work. 'Go and stand just there,' he said, 'and watch how easily it moves over, almost without a sound! My word, my ancestors were a

245

sharp lot! And to think the poor old trippers were dunned regularly to come out in boats and see a freak of Nature!'

He took my arm and marched me to a spot he considered would be good to see it work, and then he said, 'Just time it – I make it fifteen seconds to cover four and a half feet.'

How lunatic can you get, when you're in love? I still had no doubts about who I was talking to, although the touch on my arm should have told me. But it was so clever, giving me something to do, something co-operative. I fell for it, and was torn between watching the great slab of rock moved softly across a runway which must have been covered with sand before, and which he had now cleared – and watching the second hand of my watch go round. It was a luminous watch, but I still couldn't see it clearly, so I forgot his instructions and put on my torch, and in the glare I saw his face. He was leaning against the wall, clutching his shoulder, and his face was a mixture of physical pain and a terrible grin of pure amusement, no, perhaps triumphant amusement. In that second I knew that it was Nick, and not Simon.

But the rock had moved across in those split seconds, and closed, before I could even call to him, I was so stunned.

When I did find my voice, I shrieked at him to open up and let me in, but of course, he couldn't hear me through that thickness.

I jumped down on to the strip of beach that was still uncovered by the tide, and flashed my torch to see if there was any way to the top, but there not only wasn't, but I couldn't find the cave itself any more. There were any number of caves, but a cursory glance showed me that they were the little ones, and the tide ran right in them. There was no shelter there. If I didn't find a way off this strip of beach, I would be drowned, or dashed to my death by the breakers, on to the rocks.

I couldn't believe it. I stood there for a minute, thinking, getting my breath after so much fruitless running about trying to find a way out. That had been Nick, and he had deliberately tricked me into coming out here, I saw – there was nothing strange about it, either, for I knew too much about him. I knew he had sent Jimmy Noy to his death, probably the chauffeur, too, for although the chauffeur had called him 'Simon' that night, I remembered how the man had looked so sharply and stared at him in the driving mirror, when he had grandly introduced himself as Holford of Wishbourne. That must have been Nick's 'thing', just as believing in the gold was Nick's 'thing'. His trade-mark, the only way to be sure that it was Nick, with that dyed hair, and not Simon. Simon, I realized, in that flash of perception, was not likely to ever introduce himself in that grand way, nor to believe that there were riches somewhere under Wishbourne Towers for the taking.

Nick believed that, and he would kill for it. He had already, and not even made it a clean killing, but faked each instance to look like an accident. There would have been another 'accidental death' tonight, too, if Brett hadn't discovered the housemaid.

What had happened to that girl, I wondered? She should have been lying on the couch in the library, where Brett had put her while he aroused me. Undoubtedly Nick had discovered her and finished her off.

I shivered, and it occurred to me that I ought to move from that spot, because if he thought better of it and came out to see if I were still there, heaven knew what he might do.

Even as I stood there, looking up at the cliffs to where Wishbourne Towers was a great black hulk against the starlit sky, every light in the place went up, one after another.

The sea moved me on, or I would have stood there staring, wondering what had happened to have aroused the whole household. It was uncanny, those lights, first one, then another, starting downstairs and working upwards. Nick, telling them I had been drowned?

My heart beat furiously. I was so tempted to stay there, in case someone came to let down a rope but how would they know where I was, or that I was still alive?

I forced myself to think: which way did the tide move? I must think which part of the beach got covered first. Finally I reluctantly came to the conclusion that I might just save myself if I could get through to Jimmy Noy's cottage. I had climbed a few yards up one day to see if the black horse was tethered there, and it seemed to me that the tide didn't come up too high at the end of the beach. I was tempted to climb again, but didn't think I would be safe in the dark, and Nick might come out to look for me. He knew I had climbed in that spot.

I began the perilous way along the base of the cliffs, hanging on to a rock whenever the breakers came too far in, and clinging for dear life while the sea tried to suck me backwards. And to give me courage, I kept saying, over and over again, 'Simon! Simon! Simon!' Somewhere he would be looking for me and come and find me.

That idiotic piece of optimism went stale on me suddenly. I had a sudden mind picture of Simon lying asleep on that couch in the attic when Brett had shone his torch down on him. Well, if that hadn't told me anything and warned me, what would? That torch beam should have awakened him but it hadn't. Of course it hadn't – it had been Nick, lying there and shamming sleep! Then where was Simon?

I had to keep going, but my feet dragged now. All hope went. Nick had killed Simon, I was sure. What did it matter to him, with three people already on his conscience? He could have managed it, I was sure. I didn't understand the significance of the locked bedroom – for one wild moment I wondered if Nick had left Simon in there after disposing of him but I didn't think Nick would have had the strength, after losing so much blood from that shoulder wound. But I was sure I would never see Simon again.

And then, at that precise moment, when I needed hope so much, the wind dropped, and I heard the horse's hooves. Against the slightly lighter backcloth of the sky, the great black beast paused for an instant just above me, as if the rider were searching the beach. The cliff was much lower here, but too smooth and sheer for me to attempt to climb. It looked like Simon up there. I dare not be sure, but I had to make up my mind. Horse and man looked as one, and I had never heard that Nick had ridden that horse more than that one time, when he had almost ridden me down. I had to make up my mind, and an extra high breaker decided me. I don't know how I clung to that bit of rock, but when the sea had gone back again, I shouted, and showed the beam of my torch. I held my breath but he had seen me.

Simon ... or Nick? I held my breath and waited, and I don't think I ever want to go through a waiting period like that again in my life.

The sea was up to my waist when he reached me, on the end of a rope. Then I saw others up there, and I breathed again. If it was Nick he wouldn't attempt anything if he wasn't alone.

I had forgotten Nick's shoulder wound, but in any case, he had seemed to me to have superhuman strength. So I still wasn't sure until Simon briefly clutched me to him and said something that sounded like: 'Carey! Thank God we found you!'

I don't think I remember clearly what happened after that. I think he told me that the black horse was taking most of the strain of the rope. I do remember how he tried to instruct me to stand right out from the rope and 'walk' up the cliff. It seemed impossible, but he urged me so, and reminded me that he would have to stay down there until I was up.

I did my best, but there was a nasty moment when a scutter of small stones and lumps of rock fell, missing me by inches. I thought I heard a shout from below, but I reached the top then and was hauled up. The rope went down again, and we waited. Brett was there. He took me in charge, and wanted to carry me back to the house, but suddenly a chill had descended on me. 'Leave me alone!' I said. 'Why isn't he coming up? Those bits of rock that went past me – Brett, one must have hit him! Brett, it was Simon, *Simon!*'

Chapter Fifteen

I didn't want to remember that awful night for a long time afterwards. I said so to Brett, when he came back from London, three weeks later. The party he had come to the Towers with had long since departed, but we had had so much publicity since then, that there was never a moment to stand and talk. I wanted to talk to Brett so much, but there were queues of tourists to be shown around, and we had made the town boom, too. Wishbourne Towers was included in the Mystery Night Coach Trips, and everyone was suddenly so prosperous that it was somehow all wrong that there should have been such a struggle for money such a little time ago.

Lady Isadora took pity on me, and told me to take Brett out for a walk somewhere, while she escorted the latest party around.

I went, gladly. I'd had enough of showing the holidaymakers the places that had been so painful to us not so long ago.

It was a glorious day, warm enough to take

away the edge that was always on the wind that came in from the sea. Brett said, 'Can you bear to go so near the edge of the cliffs, after what happened?'

I said levelly, 'I can if you can give me definite good news of him and not just hope.'

Brett laughed shortly. 'Simon Holford has got nine lives, I should think. You would think, wouldn't you, that after one wham on the head with a bit of rock, that would be enough. But no, sir, the latest tests show that the second bit of rock did him nothing but good. Well, don't believe me, if you don't want to, but I have it from the Great Man himself that Simon Holford's sight is going to be unimpaired and he's going to be all right. And if his aunt's satisfied, everyone ought to be, including his aunt's most efficient personal and private secretary. What will you do, Carey? You won't stay here, will you?'

'No, Brett, I don't want to be here when Simon comes home. I only waited to hear that he'd be all right.'

He leaned against the new rail that had been put up on the cliff top, and looked at me. I could feel him looking at me but I kept my gaze steadily out to sea. He was going to ask me about Simon and I didn't want him to.

But he didn't, not directly. He just said mildly, 'I never expected to hear you say that. Do you mind if I ask you why you followed Nick down that night?'

'You mean you think I should have known it wasn't Simon lying on that couch up there? Did you know it wasn't Simon?'

Brett said, 'I had a hunch it wasn't. I just wanted to get down to that room again, to see why it was locked. I expected to find Simon down there but not alive and well and talking to the housemaid. When I learned that she'd come to, found herself in the library and was scared that Nick would find she wasn't dead in the cellar, she rushed upstairs to find someone else to protect her and ran slap into Nick, as she thought, going into his room, but I guess it was Simon and he was quick enough to put his hand over her mouth to stop her shouting and he locked the door to keep out the possibility of Nick's returning, while he thought what to do. He told me he guessed the only thing was to tell her there were two of them, which wasn't difficult to prove, since he hadn't got a wound on the shoulder.

'Brett, I was never so glad in my life when

255

I found that girl was all right,' I said fervently.

'Never mind about the housemaid,' Brett said. 'You still haven't told me what made you so sure that that was Simon on the couch in the attic.'

'I expected him to be there. It was arranged,' I said stiffly. I was not going to disclose any more of that intimate scene in my bedroom than I could help. 'Remember, Nick was in Simon's room – in Simon's bed – everyone thought he *was* Simon, so Simon had nowhere else to go but to the attics. And it was arranged that I should go to him there.'

'Where did you see him to talk to him?' Brett asked, and he looked rather angry, a thing which I didn't understand then.

'In the gun room. I saw him while you were sitting on Nick after you'd floored him, remember?'

'So that was why you looked so sick,' he recalled. 'Yes, it must have been quite a shock for you to discover there were two of them at that particular moment,' he said feelingly.

'And now Nick's dead,' I said, thinking. 'Tell me again about it. I think I've had everyone else's version but yours, Brett.'

'It wasn't pretty. Do you really want to hear about it again?' I nodded, adding, 'I suppose it was you who wouldn't let me hear about it that night?'

'Well, I didn't want another patient on my hands. It was enough to have to take Simon back looking in a frightful state. I don't mind telling you, Carey baby, I was sure glad to find that new wound was only superficial and that he just looked a bit of a mess.' He got out his pipe and began to pack it with tobacco while he talked. I liked the smell of his tobacco. He said, 'Simon told me where you'd be likely to be found. In the cave itself, with maybe Nick. Simon sure looked murderous. We went down, the three of us, though why the housemaid went too, I guess I can't think. She just wanted company. I kinda think she wished she'd stayed upstairs later on, when we found Nick.'

He shook his head, tried to make his pipe draw, and failed. 'It was out of this world! He'd somehow got up his step ladder. He must have been chipping away at those mended places in the ceiling of the cave – did you know how he always kept pacing and counting, across the floor of the cave? Gold there was there, he always held, and gold he'd find. And the poor fella sure found it.'

257

He lit the pipe again but the wind blew the match out so he gave it up. 'Gold there was. It just started to fall in small lots, mixed up with bits of the ceiling, then it gathered momentum. He never had time to even slide down the ladder. It just kept on falling. We tried to drag him out but it was no good. He was dead.'

'Oh, Brett, how horrible you make it sound!' I cried.

'It's what we all kept saying afterwards. Gold he meant to have, and it just rained gold on him. Those old ancestors knew a thing or two, bricking it up in the roof of the cave, but it should have been gone about in a scientific way, not just hacking at it from right underneath.'

He put the pipe away. 'Then Simon went mad. He realized the gate was shut. It seems the housemaid found out about it from Nick which was why he thought she'd have to go. She showed Simon where the switch was to close it but she never found out how to open it. Simon got it into his head that you'd been shut out on the beach. I must admit I couldn't bring myself to think you'd go willingly out there. I thought maybe Nick had got rough with you and you were unconscious. Well, we shot back into the house and put all the lights on and roused the place to get help. You know the rest.'

I nodded. 'Yes, I know the rest. But even Percy's story in the papers wasn't quite as graphic as your eye witness account of what happened in the Cave of Gold.'

'Oh, Percy got it, did he? Well, I'm glad about that. I guess he deserved it, after the way he was so shamefully treated over that first fake haunting,' Brett said.

We laughed. 'No-one took umbrage, you know. We covered our tracks, it seemed, and gave good entertainment value.'

'Yes, but I sure am surprised to find Wishbourne flung open to the public. I would have thought Lady Isadora would have wanted to keep in the background, after such goings on. After all, she's got enough money, with all the gold being found.'

'It's Simon's,' I said shortly. 'After Nick's death Simon's the next to inherit.'

'Oh, I see,' he said.

'No, you don't see at all,' I said angrily. 'I'm quite sure Simon will want to share it out between his aunt and uncles. He's like that. But for the moment, they still need the money.'

'What, what the tourists bring in?'

'I think they like the publicity, too. They're

tremendously proud of Wishbourne,' I had to admit.

'And you, Carey? What will become of you?' he asked me.

'That's up to Lady Isadora, and at the moment she's giving me more than I can cope with. What about you, Brett? Are you going back to the States?'

'Not me!' he said, laughing, though his eyes still looked searchingly at me. 'I'm going to stick around in case a real ghost decides to turn up.'

'What, stay at Wishbourne Towers?' Dismay must have been in my voice. I didn't want Miss Kidby upset any more by the sudden advent of another guest after all that had happened.

'No, though I may visit, Lady Isadora tells me, when I wish. No, I shall stay in the village. It's a good inn there, they tell me. And then I shall go back to London to fetch Simon when he's fit to travel.'

'You'll let me know when that will be, won't you?' I asked quickly. 'I mean, I'd want time to pack and go. I don't want to meet him again.'

I fancied Brett looked pleased, as he assured me he would do that. Meantime he said he was going to see that I got taken out and given fresh air, after all I had been through.

Lady Isadora approved of this. She said, the next day, when Brett was to come and drive me into Migstanton for dinner at the Star and Garter there, 'He likes you, Carey.'

'He likes everyone, I think, ma'am,' I said lightly.

She looked bothered. 'About what happened, child,' she began, but I didn't want to talk about it.

'It's all put behind me,' I broke in. 'I wish you wouldn't mention it again, please. I wish you would forget any confidences I gave you, too, concerning for instance, how I could tell between Simon and Nick. It doesn't matter any more, truly it doesn't.'

'Then it wasn't what is, I believed, known as The Real Thing?' she asked painfully.

'That doesn't matter any more, either,' I said. 'The thing is, Simon's going to be all right. He won't lose his sight, and he'll be *all right.*'

'Yes, but what will you do when he comes home, child?'

'What would you like me to do, ma'am?' I asked her directly.

'Well, it all depends on what Simon wants us to do. If he's going to arrange for us –

myself and his uncles – to stay on here, and if he doesn't object to our activities regarding the public, then we shall need your excellent clerical services, but will you want to stay? Or are you going to be like the rest, and feel you must move on to something less tame? Because, you know, we can't promise any more hauntings – I'm afraid we've played that out.'

'You don't believe there really *is* a ghost, ma'am?'

She was evasive. 'I don't know, Carey, and sometimes I'm rather ashamed of descending to the vulgar, in exposing our secrets to the public eye, just to get money. I ought never to have let people go through the panel and down to the cave. I ought to have closed it, I suppose, since poor Nick...'

Poor Nick was a bad young man, I thought grimly, but there it was. He was a Holford, and so was she, and that was how her thoughts ran.

'Well,' she said, with a smile, 'What will you do? Stay on with us and work as well as you've always done?'

I begged her to let me leave it for a while. I knew what I was going to do, but I also knew that if I disclosed that I was going to run away before Simon's return, she would keep on about it. I don't believe she wanted me to marry Simon, but it would have been on her conscience.

A visitor for me, that day, rather altered things a little. Percy Drewett arrived.

He stood there, in the doorway of the library, leaning on the lintel, as usual, his felt hat at a rakish angle, his raincoat stained, flying open, of course, and a very, very casual sort of sweater over unpressed slacks. After Simon's impeccable tailoring, and Brett's quite presentable appearance, Percy really looked very untidy.

But nice. He smiled slowly, delightedly, and said softly, 'Hello. How's tricks?'

'Percy!' I exclaimed. 'What are *you* doing down here? Your paper sent you for another story?' I went forward with my hand outstretched, to shake his, unfeigned delight in my voice. I was very pleased with Percy. I had felt for some time that he behaved very well all round, all things considered.

'No. I'm on holiday. Well, even chaps like me get a holiday sometimes. And Lady Thingummy said I could take you off for the day if I could get you to agree.'

'Did she? Well, that's very tiresome of her, because she already loaded me up with work and she knows very well that Dr Pilkington is taking me out to dinner tonight.'

Percy blinked. 'Oh, that chap still hanging around? Like him, Carey?'

'Well, you know what he did for us all, and we all like him,' I said warmly.

'Not what I asked, is it?' he said, and stared at me with that searching look that Brett had sometimes.

'Well, why are you asking?' I demanded wrathfully. 'And for goodness sake come in out of that open doorway and shut it.'

He did, and came and sat on the corner of my desk. 'Do you like him specially?' he persisted.

'Brett Pilkington? I never thought of it,' I said, frowning, and I didn't attempt to then, either. It didn't seem worth it. I said to Percy, 'You *are* on the track of a new story, aren't you?'

'Always on that, love,' he assured me seriously. 'Whole life given up to it. Always will be like that. Do you know,' he said, leaning towards me, 'at my sister's wedding, which I was covering, I saw something odd go past the window and I ran out and got my first big chance, and I forgot all about the wedding and they had to find another best man?'

'I think that's awful!' I said. 'At least, I

would if I believed it,' and we both started to laugh.

'Lunch time,' he announced. 'Come down to the village. Good pub there. Lady Isadora says you can.'

'I am starving,' I allowed, 'but I must check with her first.' But of course, I might have known that Percy really had got permission. We went out to a really smart car. 'Not yours?' I said.

'No point in getting a lift here any more,' he said, with a funny smile. 'No more ghosts, no more deaths.'

'No, you've got it wrong,' I hastened to correct him, as I got into his car. 'It's *disaster* that comes with the Candles.'

'Wouldn't you call accidental death a disaster?' he queried.

'It's only a part of disaster, which could be losing all your money, or anything, couldn't it?'

'You're quibbling,' he told me, 'but I accept your correction, ma'am. Do you like me?'

'Well, of course I do, silly,' I said, and he let it rest there until we had eaten. We had a very good lunch. Steak done just as I liked it, and a very good wine to go with it. Without his disreputable hat and raincoat, he looked rather nice. Cosy. He told me a lot about the sort of food he liked, and I found I shared most of his tastes. I liked some of the wine he mentioned, but hadn't really had much chance to try them. And I hadn't travelled at all.

'Want to?' he asked, experimentally.

'As what?' The suspicion was thick in my voice. 'Or is it just a job you are offering me?'

'You could say that,' he said, on consideration.

He wouldn't discuss it any more until we had left the pub and were in his car again. He talked about his job and what a roving life he had, and that if he ever married, it would have to be to a girl who was adventurous, had plenty of spirit and courage, and never wanted to stay put. 'Like you, Carey,' he added.

I was utterly dismayed. I hadn't thought that this very odd conversation would be leading up to an offer of marriage. Goodness, poor Percy struck me as being the last type of fellow to want to saddle himself with a wife.

'You can't be serious?' I protested. 'It *is* just a job you have lined up for me, isn't it?'

'No,' he said flatly. 'It isn't, and you know it. We've talked before, Carey. We spent a good deal of time together when I was collecting material for that first story. I thought we understood each other. You must know that a chap only talks about himself when he wants a girl to, well, to consider him. Dash it, I thought it would be easy to ask you while I was driving, and you being a sensible girl, you'd know damn well what I was asking you for. I want you to marry me.'

'Oh, Percy, why did you have to spoil it?' I could have cried. 'I was so pleased to see you and I thought we'd always be friends, perhaps even work together.'

'Well, it would come to that, if you married me,' he said casually. 'I told you how I ran out on my sister's wedding. I'd probably run out on my wife, too, and I'd expect you to pack up and come after me. I'm no lady's man, you know. It's Holford's style to go down on one knee and make a speech–'

'Leave him out of it!' I snapped.

'Oh. It's like that, is it,' he murmured, and he was silent for some time.

'I'm sorry, Percy. Didn't mean to snap at you. The fact is, I don't suppose I shall marry anyone. I'd never feel comfortable, not knowing who my parents were, you know. How could I be expected to?'

'That's understandable if you've got your

cap set at Holford, but me, I wouldn't bother about such a trifle. It would be you who counted, Carey, when I thought of anyone at all, that is. We'd have fun, and we'd globetrot, and I thought you'd be sensible enough to know that my job came first, every time.'

'I don't think I could settle for that,' I said, in a stifled voice. 'Please, Percy, as I don't know anything about my past, let's leave it.'

He looked so hurt, but he got me back in good time for my evening date with Brett Pilkington. I had forgotten about it but Percy hadn't. Never did I feel less like going out to dinner with anyone.

'You go out and have fun and forget about me,' Percy said. 'I'll survive. But be careful of Pilkington – he's a bad loser. And that reminds me. I brought something for you, and you might as well have it, even though you have said a most emphatic no,' and he began to struggle with a back pocket. 'Oh, damn, I can't get it. Never mind, remind me to give it to you when we get back to Wishbourne.'

He forgot it, and so did I, because Lady Isadora was in the hall, and she embarrassed me very much by saying archly, 'Well, Percy, have you stolen my secretary from me? Remember what I said – you must find me a new one at once if you have.'

Percy said, rather frigidly, I thought, 'I haven't, ma'am,' and though he stood there listening apparently politely to her flow of small talk, I could see he wasn't listening to a word.

I was glad when he went. I think he wanted to kiss me, but Lady Isadora didn't leave us, which was a pity.

Almost at once Brett Pilkington arrived. He didn't look very pleased.

Lady Isadora said, 'Ah, dear Dr Pilkington, do join us for drinks while that naughty girl is shaking off the dust of an adventurous afternoon with Fleet Street,' and she bore him off with her to the drawing room.

I went and had a quick bath and put on my one good dress and wished I could think of a way of getting out of it, but I couldn't.

Brett's idea of a meal out with a girl was to present her with a transparent florist box, and have the head waiter dancing attendance, a table near enough to hear the music, without its being so loud as to drown one's conversation, and to take a long time considering the wine. There was dancing, too. He was a slick operator, I will say that for him, and he did make me enjoy the evening up to a point. His conversation was interesting, too, in that slow Southern drawl of his, and he told me about his home and his family, which was a large one, and about his grandmother, who was a little old lady with such dignity that people after meeting her for the first time, came away with the impression that she was much taller.

Brett was not hard up. Without being crude enough to put it into words, he painted a picture of a cosseted wife he would have one day, who wanted for nothing. Like Percy, he couldn't resist mentioning Simon, however, to see how I reacted, I suppose.

'We are an old family,' he told me seriously. 'Not an aristocratic one like the Holfords, and we do not live in a castle–'

'Wishbourne isn't a castle,' I said fiercely.

'My, you sure do get touchy when that family and their home is mentioned, Carey. You sure you're not still after him?'

'I never was after him, as you put it,' I said, 'and you know very well that as soon as I know he's coming back, I shall leave. You promised me you'd let me know, Brett.'

'Right, so you don't wanna marry Holford and I understand you very rightly turned the reporter down today. The cheek of the fellow!'

'Percy is a very nice person,' I said crossly,

'but I don't want to marry anyone.'

He paused, for effect, I think. 'Not even me, Carey, if I was to ask you?'

'You wouldn't ask me, Brett, because I'm quite sure a grandmother such as you have, would not approve of me at all.'

'She wouldn't see you much,' he assured me, 'and anyway, I'm her favourite grandson, and we'd live in New York City, in a swell apartment most of the time, just moving out for vacation, and you'd have servants and furs and jewels and all the things you've wanted,' he said earnestly.

'You don't know what I want,' I said softly.

'Oh, yes, I do, because you're a very natural girl and all girls like pretty things. But you're a very special girl because you're not pretty and you don't give the eye yet all the boys look at you that way, you know? It's called allure, I believe.'

'Oh, don't be silly, Brett,' I said crossly.

'And that, too. You don't prink and perk and act all girlish, you just bite a fellow's head off and then he knows where he is. I guess you'd be the kind of wife to stand by a fellow through thick and thin.'

'Yes, I would,' I agreed, 'if I married anyone, which I won't, and I've told you why, Brett, and nothing in the world will alter that. I couldn't risk marrying anyone, Brett, because if one of my children turned out to be, well, say like Nick, poor Nick – I wouldn't be at all surprised if my husband blamed me, because he didn't know what sort of roots I sprang from. And don't you say it doesn't matter. It does, oh, it truly does.'

And after that, of course, there was nothing else for it but to ask him to take me home.

He went, the next day, though nobody told me. It was a wet day, and the tourists flocked in. A storm drove them up by the coach loads. They painstakingly tramped upstairs and down, between the roped off sections, looking solemnly at the big table where the Candles were supposed to appear, and up to the attics where the original candelabra hung, still festooned with dust and cobwebs. Down through the little panel, to the cave, and an extra fee to see the stone close up. Sir Hilton did this part of it, while I and Lady Isadora took batches of people over the well-worn path. I had learned a certain amount of patter about Holfords in the past, but I hated reciting it, and I hated still more the impertinent questions that sightseers put to us. Someone had just asked if she could see the gold that fell from the cave roof, and someone else said it ought to be put in a glass case to prove there ever was any. Someone else asked what it was worth, and then, as I indignantly raised my head to answer that one, I stared right into the face of Simon.

It was such a shock. He looked very pale, as one would expect, just coming out of hospital, and there was Brett behind him, sardonically smiling, taking in, I suppose, all the personal and private emotions suddenly laid bare in my face, because I was taken by surprise.

'Simon!' I heard myself whisper it. I couldn't stop myself. He said coolly, 'Good afternoon, Carey,' and then, to the people just standing stupidly staring, he said, 'Excuse me,' in a murmur, and passed through and up the grand staircase, Brett behind him.

I didn't think of it at the time – I thought Simon was being formal because of all those strangers around – but later, when I was alone, and Simon appeared and was just as formal, I remembered belatedly Percy's remark about Brett being a bad loser.

I couldn't think what the significance of it was at the time, however. I only knew Brett must have said something to make Simon look at me like that: as if I were a stranger, one he didn't care for.

I was heartbroken. I would never forgive Brett for not keeping his promise to warn me when Simon was returning. I could have remembered Simon that night in my room, kissing me, telling me there was nobody else, and later proving it by risking his life to save me. No, Brett wasn't content to lose; he had to spoil even my memories.

I asked Lady Isadora if I could be released at once. It was the quiet ten minutes before she went down for cocktails. 'Have you gone mad, Carey? Of course I won't release you! We're run off our legs, and now Simon has come back, and you want to go. Don't be silly!'

'I shall go, tomorrow, Lady Isadora, but I would prefer it if you gave me permission to go,' I said.

'Don't be selfish, Carey. Get me someone else as good as you, and you can leave on the instant,' was all she would say.

Simmering with anger, I went up to my room and began packing. But after I had had my meal, on a tray, and paused for reflection, I knew I couldn't go without finishing all that typing. And the typewriter was down in the library. Well, I must wait till the household had gone to bed, I supposed. So I did. I lay on my bed with a book, waiting, and I suppose I must have dropped off to sleep.

When I awoke, the phosphorescent hands of my clock pointed to two in the morning. I jumped up annoyed with having wasted at least an hour and taking a torch, went quietly downstairs.

Half way down, I halted, puzzled. I had done this trip time and again, in the past, when the household had been asleep.

Now I was cold, chilled to the marrow, and it struck me that the house was brooding, unfriendly. I hadn't come down in the small hours since Nick had died, and the gold had been found, and I had the queer fancy that Nick's angry spirit was still around.

I braced my shoulders angrily. I was cold, of course, after having fallen to sleep fully dressed on the bed, and then come down to a chilled house in the small hours. That was all.

But I couldn't shake off the wretched despondent feeling, and when I had almost reached the library door, something made me turn round. Turn to look at the great central table where the Candles were supposed to appear. And there they were.

At least, it was a great gold blur of light, with the vague shape of candles and their stand. I remember I gasped. Nothing more. Just a great gasp of terror and I stood shaking, ice-cold.

Someone came to the library door and opened it, and a great slant of electric light came out, stabbing the darkness of the hall. Simon stood there, in a figured silk dressing-gown over his day clothes, a book in his hand.

'Carey?' he ejaculated, stepping forward.

I could only point dumbly, and pointed to the table. 'The Candles!' That was all I could say, and I fled to his arms, without thinking. He held me tightly, comforting me.

'Where, love, where?' he murmured, and when I pointed to the table, he reached round and flooded the hall with light. There was nothing there, except a vague shape of mist or fog, and then that went. I said, 'Put the light out again,' and he did, and there was just a vague something, which in turn vanished. And it was so icy cold.

Simon said, 'You're perished, and shaking like a leaf. Come in here in the warm. There's nothing out here.'

'But didn't you see the Candles?' I asked

him anxiously. I began for one awful moment, to fear for my reason.

'There seemed to be a sort of mist patch,' he allowed slowly, 'but I may have been mistaken. Why aren't you undressed and fast asleep in bed?'

I told him, impatiently, 'I couldn't leave with all that work undone, but I fell asleep. It's so cold out there in the hall. I *must* have been–'

'The heating failed, my aunt told me,' he soothed me. 'What's this about you leaving? Are you marrying so soon?' he frowned.

'Marrying? I'm not marrying,' I said. 'I'm just leaving. I don't want to stay here.'

'Why not?' he asked very quietly.

I couldn't tell him. 'What made you think I was marrying?'

Still frowning, he said, 'That's odd. I understood from Pilkington that you were marrying that reporter chap who came here at first.'

'Brett! That's funny, Percy said take care because Brett was a bad loser,' and I was going on to explain, when the tears started to flow. I was furious. Isn't it marvellous? Whenever I want to explain a situation I don't like, I start to bawl – good old Carey Constable, start to bellow right away! I was so cross, I turned away from him, and searched for my hankie, dropping my notebook, my torch, my pen, the lot. Then I found I hadn't got a hankie on me.

'Turn round,' Simon said, with resignation, and efficiently mopped my face, then he crushed me in an embrace that knocked the breath out of my body, and when he came up for air, he said, 'Don't go. Don't go, Carey, you can't. I've been living for the day when I'd see you again. When Pilkington told me you'd fixed it up with the reporter yesterday I took a body blow. I didn't know what to do.'

'It wasn't fair,' I choked. 'I'd turned Percy down. I'd turned Brett down–'

'Pilkington proposed to you himself?' Simon demanded, and then he started to laugh, softly. 'So that was what it was all about! My love, you have good sense!'

'You don't understand, Simon. I'm not going to marry anyone,' and I made the same old explanation over again.

Simon said, 'Let's sit down and talk about it,' and the letters didn't get typed. We talked; fruitlessly, but it was heavenly. He said it didn't matter to him who I was, but I knew better. But in the end I just let him talk. We talked about what happened the night Nick died, and Simon went over all the scenes I had had with Nick, until he was sure that he knew everything, and that Nick had only kissed me two or three times. He hated the thought but he had to satisfy himself that it was no worse, and he had to be sure that neither Brett nor Percy had ever kissed me. And then he kissed me.

'We're going to be married,' he pronounced. 'Quietly, no fuss. Just Aunt Isadora and the uncles. And we'll have a nice modern flat somewhere – London or Paris or perhaps in Rome. You say what you'd like. But we won't live here.'

I lifted a face that was shining, I know, though I knew it was make-believe. I knew I wouldn't marry him, not knowing about myself, but it was heavenly to know I wouldn't have to live at Wishbourne. 'You *did* see it just now, didn't you, Simon? You do believe there *is* a ghost?'

'I don't know, my love. I could persuade myself I saw something. I know you believe you saw something. I know you would never be happy here. I know I couldn't be, if you weren't happy. Besides, there are too many unhappy memories connected with the place. No, I think I am tempted to give Wishbourne Towers to the nation, wash my hands of it.'

'But your aunts and uncles love it so,' I reminded him.

'They say they do,' he murmured. 'I wonder how deep that feeling goes? I just wonder what they'd do with a quarter of the gold to play with? Probably make tracks for Paris, because of Longchamps. Well, it would be the races somewhere,' he smiled. 'As for me, I've got a notion I'd like to go into business. No, not racing horses, but breeding them. How say you, my love?' and he kissed me again.

I wasn't going to argue. I did ask him nervously what I would say to Brett the next day, but he assured me that Brett had gone, late tonight. 'All things considered, it's as well,' he said, and insisted that I went straight to bed.

I dreamed of Simon, holding his arms out to me, but some inexplicable force pulling me backwards away from him, and then with the grey light of dawn, I slid into a dreamless sleep, and nobody woke me. When I did get up, shocked that I should have overslept so, it was to be told that someone was on the telephone for me.

I took it in the library and while I was speaking, Simon came in, smiling as if everything in the world was all right.

It was Percy on the telephone. 'What do *you* want?' I asked him, crossly. I was so afraid he had got wind of what I had seen last night and I didn't want him or any other reporters questioning me, not any more.

'Sorry, love, to bother you,' he said. 'Promised myself I wouldn't speak to you again, but I can't get out of my mind the nagging doubt that you might not have received it. I mean stands to reason, if you had, the announcement should be in the jolly old Marriages Column.'

'Percy, what *are* you talking about?' I asked, exasperated, so Simon quietly took the receiver from me and dealt with it.

He listened to Percy, and said composedly, 'Yes, she certainly is. Yes, indeed, we are. No, not yet. It was only decided late last night. Pilkington? No, he went, before that.'

I tugged at Simon's arm to stop him before he said too much, but he moved away, smiling at me, and went on listening to Percy. 'Well, I'd like to give it to you, old chap, but it'll be a very quiet affair. However, we may have something more for you later,' and covering the receiver, he murmured to me, 'We can let him have the item about abandoning Wishbourne, can't we?'

I shook my head fiercely, but he took no notice, and then his face lit and he got very interested in what Percy was saying. 'Did he! Well, that's confoundedly decent of you, Drewett, and I can't thank you enough. You'll be hearing from us! Yes, yes, it's made all the difference – to Carey, anyway.'

I waited with ill concealed impatience for all the greetings to finish, the promises and the goodbyes, and finally he put the telephone down and turned to me. 'He promised to give you something, and he forgot but met Pilkington on the way up and asked him to deliver it. Of course, Pilkington did no such thing!' Simon said grimly.

'Oh, must I accept a present from Percy?' I whispered.

'Yes, you must, my love. It comes with all his love and you'll treasure it. It's the information you've deplored not having – about who you are! Well, newspaper chap, access to all the records, he's found out the lot.'

I backed away a little. I couldn't believe it and now it had actually come, I wasn't sure I wanted to know.

But I need not have worried. 'Your father was a doctor, local G.P. and your mother a nurse. Now, nothing very exceptional in that, is there? Drewett's got a copy of your birth certificate. I daresay Pilkington's burnt it but Drewett promised to get another. It's a gift from the heart, my dear, so accept it graciously.'

'Oh, Simon!' and for once I didn't cry. I was beyond that. 'But why, why did my – my foster-mother – make such a mystery of it, and let that horrible man tell me, like that?' I exploded.

'It was because of him, it seems. It seemed likely that you'd marry soon and she wanted to be settled, and that man suited her, but he was a jealous type, and he'd hardly care to hear that she'd brought up the daughter of the man she had been in love with once, when he and his wife died on the job, in a factory explosion. She had always meant to tell you, but put it off too long. As it was, Drewett, in seeing her, wasn't allowed in the house. It seems they haven't gone to Canada yet. He met her in a tea-shop. He wants you to know that she sends her love.' Simon forced himself to add, 'And Drewett sends his – I suppose I must add that!'

'Oh, Simon,' I said, between tears and laughter.

'And I, my love, give you mine,' he said, as he took me into his arms.

The publishers hope that this book has given you enjoyable reading. Large Print Books are especially designed to be as easy to see and hold as possible. If you wish a complete list of our books please ask at your local library or write directly to:

Dales Large Print Books
Magna House, Long Preston,
Skipton, North Yorkshire.
BD23 4ND